Quickening

# Quickening

## Terry Griggs

The Porcupine's Quill

CANADIAN CATALOGUING IN PUBLICATION DATA

Griggs, Terry.
  Quickening

ISBN 0-88984-111-X

I. Title.

PS8563.R5365Q5 1990    C813'.54    C90-095500-7
PR9199.3.G753Q5 1990

Published by The Porcupine's Quill, Inc., 68 Main Street, Erin,
Ontario NOB 1TO with financial assistance from the Canada
Council and the Ontario Arts Council.

Distributed by The University of Toronto Press, 5201 Dufferin
Street, Downsview, Ontario M3H 5T8.

Readied for the press by John Metcalf.
Copyedited by Doris Cowan.

Cover is after a photograph by Tony Urquhart.

Printed and bound by The Porcupine's Quill.
The stock is Zephyr laid, and the type, Ehrhardt.

Many thanks to Jan Zwicky, Jane Urquhart, and my editor, John Metcalf, who have given so generously their time, insights, and encouragement. I would also particularly like to thank David Burr, my first and most loyal reader, and Stan Dragland, who has been subjected to these stories and others, even worse, for years.

I am indebted to Frank A. Meyers for his interviews with Manitoulin pioneers and members of the Obidgewong band, to Allan Dryburgh for his delightful reminiscences published in *The Manitoulin Expositor*, and especially to my father, John Griggs, for his wealth of stories and his art in the telling.

As well, I want to express my appreciation for the financial support received from the Explorations Programme of the Canada Council, the Ontario Arts Council, and the City of London.

# Contents

'Islands are also secret places, where the unconscious grows conscious, where possibilities mushroom, where imagination never rests.' *John Fowles*

\*

For David and Sandy Galen

# Suddenly

Went, I mean.

Snowflakes streaking past our eyes, stars jiggling up there in the sky.

*Foop*, into the snowbank.

Buck was laughing to split a gut, and he said, 'Marsha, you're a kook,' and I suppose he was right, considering. *'Exhilarator! Haw, haw.'* He was smacking his hand on the dashboard. Did I say that? I expect I did. You know, words zip out of my mouth assbackwards half the time. Like then, when I hit the, excuse me, *accelerator* instead of the brakes and couldn't even get the swearing right. Probably because I was trying to pray at the same time, 'Holy Shitface Mother of Bob, not the fender, please not the headlights.' What we're talking about here is Daddy's brand new Comet GT with the Luxury Decor Option – cut-pile carpeting, colour-keyed vinyl roof and wheel covers, reclining contoured bucket seats – all the spiffy features Daddy couldn't stop jawing about that I'd just parked in a huge fucking snowbank.

'Shut up, Buck!' Though I shouldn't have said that, either. Way to impress a guy, eh?

I'd been working on it, too. 'It' being Buck and me, somewhere alone. Not in a snowbank, I'll admit. That wasn't exactly what I was after. Getting my mitts on Daddy's car hadn't been easy. Getting Buck *in it* hadn't been easy. He's had his mind, such as it is, on other things lately. *Two* things, Trudy's, and they keep changing sizes, that's the joke. I nearly had to run him over. 'Hey, Buckaroo, wanna go for a ride?'

What I wanted from Buck was simple. I wanted his undying love, his thrashing gushing heart in my hand (no matter it was likely cold and blue as a ball of ice), and I wanted to sing in his band, the Tomcats, New Year's Eve at the Lantern. I wanted this pretty bad. Feature me down on my knees every night: *Listen up,*

*Bob, you gotta do this for me. I'll wear my black dress, the one I bought in Reitman's in Sudbury with the ruffles around the hem tickling my kneecaps. Hot stuff, or what? I promise I'll be buried in it. You set me up and I'll do the rest.*

Trudy's not the only one, I've got two big things as well. One of them's my nose, you can forget about that. The other's my voice. I may not be able to talk straight, but I can sing like a siren. I could turn your ears inside out given half a chance.

Buck wasn't saying too much by then, except for, 'Shove over, will ya. I'll gun it, *you* get out and push.'

IN MEDIAS RES. (Hey, I've studied Latin.) Even the long death of high school has its moments, and here was one: Biology, we're doing cows, if you can believe it. Some farm kid's brought one into class divvied up in about four or five green garbage bags. I think I'm going to be sick. I've got the lyrics of 'Johnny Angel' running nonstop through my head like a purring engine to keep me from keeling over. Buck is sitting behind Trudy, as per usual, fanaticizing (you got it) about her swively hips, her ample tailpiece smothering the lab stool that with luck could be his face, I know he's thinking. His hand darts out and sinks into pink angora. He hooks a finger around her bra at the back and pulls it out like a sling shot. Lets it go and *snap!* Funny? Everybody turns to smirk at Trudy and even Mr. Dandy, who floats at the front of the room like he's pickled in formaldehyde, seems to wake up. You bet I was thrilled to see how embarrassed she was. No sympathy here. She got all red and hot looking and her scalp – under that teased bottle-blond hair, a French's mustard colour – kind of lit up like a lamp.

'What *was* that noise, Miss Vinney?' Dandy asks, stunned, like he's got a mouth full of acorns, and the whole class breaks up. Then damned if he doesn't steal the show himself by getting all flustered and blowing his nose on his tie.

JUST LIKE *that.* Gone. What a weird winter. Ever since I rammed into that bank, it never stopped snowing, like I ripped something open. Buckets of the stuff on the roof of the Comet by the time the tow truck got there. Thought Daddy was gonna have my hands and feet cut off, but he got over it. Frigging cold walk into town too, Buck whining and bellyaching the whole way. Think that asshole would give me a little squeeze to keep me warm? So *cold*, mercury dropped clean out of sight, and Grampy went with it. Down into shadowland. Hope the devils are taking care of him. Hope they hold his hand when he's scared like I never did. No cloud elevator up to heaven for him, he was tied to the bed. Nurses caught him sneaking down the stairs. One time, hiding in the laundry room, looking for the chute out. He was scrappy, desperate, trying to escape with his life. But that was against the rules. They tied him to the bed, and you know, death came into that room like a doctor to take his mind apart piece by piece. *Crazy as a louse*, is what he said, memories unstuck and rattling free in his head, but he knew me. 'Sing to me, sweetie, sing that one about the girl wants to get laid.' Ha, my theme song. And then, 'Look there!' He meant the spiders and scorpions crawling all over the walls. Then, 'On the floor, see! A twenty-dollar bill! Quick, pick it up!' And I stooped to snatch it up, even if it was nothing but dust. And I slipped it into my pocket. I'm saving it for shadowland. I'll spend it when I get there. I'll buy Grampy a pitchfork.

SWITCHING GEARS. *Rnnnnnnnn, RNNNNNNNNNNN!* My brother Robbie drives a kitchen chair at the supper table, making us press our fists into our temples and wish (*oh please*) that we belonged to some other family, even the Horelys down the street, not known for their brainpower. It's hard to say, but from the sounds of it, Robbie's chair has a souped-up v8 engine, four-on-the-floor, buns in the back and no muffler. He lays rubber on the checkerboard linoleum, and Mom says, 'Don't let your supper get cold, dear,' her wispy voice gobbled up by the sound of screeching brakes. I've got the sneaking suspicion he's going to hit a snowbank soon. Likes to remind Daddy about that, and to tell the truth, Daddy doesn't need reminding. He's still pissed off, though the Comet came through it, tow truck and all, without a scratch. A wonder, I'd say. And do I get thanks? Daddy dangles the car keys in front of my eyes like a silver lure then snatches them away. (Jerk.) Robbie parks by his plate, sticks a baked potato in his mouth, and says (we think), 'Deer eat birds, ya know. No guff, me and Billy were down by the banding station, and like there's these deer munching on some chickadees caught in the banding nets. And the game warden's hopping up and down flapping his arms trying to make them stop, and they don't seem scared or nothing. He says one starts and the rest of them get the idea, eh. Like some of the birds are covered in spit cause they lick 'em first, and alls that's left of some's just legs and guts and stuff. Neat, eh?'

Daddy and me stare at Robbie like he's got antlers growing out of his head, and Mom says, 'Not at the supper table, dear.' So Robbie backs up his chair, puts it in gear, and drives away.

A LANGUAGE LANDSLIDE. An avalanche, out the words tumble slam bang and razzle dazzle. Now, a song'll come out in a nice flowing stream, but my sentences hit bottom like they've been dumped out of a truck. 'A pig's breakfast,' Grampy said, but he didn't care, he loved me anyway. Likely his fault, mind you, teaching me all those cuss words when I was a baby just learning to speak, and Daddy would give me a little slap on the lips every time I said one. Didn't hurt much, but I think it made the words kind of flip out of shape. Like they had to put on disguises before sneaking out of my mouth to try the air. I remember this one time I invited a boy to a wedding conception, when what I meant to say was *reception* of course, and d'you think I've been able to live that one down? So okay, my talk's pocked and pitted but I try to fill in the blanks as best I can. I don't know, I used to have a rough time in catechism class. Nuns, cripes, they got muscles like stevedores under those black habits, and they're always after you.

'Who made the world?' they'd want to know.

'Bob made the world.'

'*Who?*'

'Bob. You know, big guy in the sky, he did it.'

Their eyes would go small and hard as dimes. 'Don't get smart with us, girl.'

BUCK. 'Oooooooo, baby.' This is his favourite saying, according to the legend under his picture in the high-school yearbook. We're wondering what's happened to those other favourites of his, 'Tough titty,' and 'Chuck you, Farles.' His ambition, we discover, is to be an 'electronic technician for female robots.' His pet peeve: 'Girls who drive.' Very funny. His hobbies and interests are listed as hockey, hunting, playing with his band, and a 'certain blonde in grade eleven-five.' Also very funny. We're dying of amusement, my better, smarter self and I.

'How's Turdy?' I ask Buck when I see him downtown.

'Name's Trudy, Dingbat.'

'Name's Marsha, Dipstick.'

'So, been drivin' much lately, huh? "(Snicker, snicker.)" Got yer snow tires on yet?'

I laugh.

Like the Queen, I might add. Far above it all.

We gaze (leer?) at Buck's picture in the yearbook. Insolent, would you say? Greasy hood-black hair tossed into a wavy heap, the look on his handsome mug suggesting nothing but harm. We hate to admit it, but we have kissed this face – the Dobermann eyes, the loverboy lips – slobbered on it until the paper buckled. And even soggy, bloated, drowned in ardour and rescued with the hose of a hair dryer, this face makes us clutch our common crotch in agony. It makes us brood (breed?), especially our feistier, more intelligent side, fretting over what kind of life we're going to have if we fall so easily for faces like this attached to pricks like him.

'Oooooooo, baby,' we croon, helpless and doe-eyed, unable to stop looking at it, even though *my* favourite saying, according to the yearbook, is: 'Get outa here, I didn't say *that*, did I?'

THE SKY opened up and out it came. Sleet, blizzards, high notes, sour notes. A regular opera of weather. Valkyries were striding along the streets kneecapping old biddies and butting them into walls. A chorus of wind was hustling people this way, that way, snow piled on their heads like wigs, vapour vines twisting like white hair out of their noses.

There was this soprano wailing and moaning in our chimney. So Daddy cocks an ear, like he does when he hears a high class singer on the radio, and says, 'Whoa, that one's gonna lay an egg soon,' culture and humour somehow inseparable in our family. Robbie thinks he's Elmer Fudd, leaping off the couch singing, 'Kill the wabbit, kill the wabbit,' and shooting things with his finger. Mom sits by the fire, knitting and humming, humming and knitting. Robbie blows a hole through her head, and she says, 'Can't you children find something to do?'

Sometimes Robbie plays dead in his room, lying on his bed for hours, stiff as a board, eyes glazed, until Mom finally discovers him and comes screaming out. At the moment he's pretending to be alive, his adolescent engine flooded with hormones. I ask him if he thinks Trudy Vinney is cute and he answers by letting his tongue unroll like a rug and flop onto his chin. I'm trying to figure out how I can sneak strychnine into her blood sausage at lunch. Her father's a butcher, you know Vinney's Meats. She's a walking advertisement, as far as I'm concerned. Under those tight stretch pants of hers I'd swear she has an economy pack of pork chops strapped to each thigh. Robbie gets his tongue back into his mouth, and says, 'Hey, did ya know Buck asked *her* to sing with the Tomcats on New Year's?'

Okay, that's it for me, folks. Madam Butterfly bites the dust. And here I thought I was in a comedy.

HE'S BACK. Hissing in my ear. *Buck don't know dickall about singing, honey, he thinks scat is somethin' you step in.* 'Oh, Grampy,' I sigh, 'either it's you, or I'm going nuts.' This more likely as I haven't slept in days. Haven't eaten. Been overdosing on what passes for drugs in this house – Vicks cough drops and baby aspirin. But I am sorely tempted to listen. It's hard to keep a bad old man down, even in hell. *Houdini,* they nicknamed him in the hospital. One nurse there, her old man a sailor, used to tie him up in blood knots and monkey's fists, and Grampy still got out of them. By the end, they had him battened down so tight it looked like he was made of rope.

*Steal the keys,* he whispers, *let's go for a little joyride. You and me, like we used to. C'mon I wanna fly. Can't get these Bobdamn wings they give me to work.*

'Shoot! That's a dead giveaway Grampy. For a minute there I thought it really was you.'

Three pairs of eyes, wide as wheels, are focused on me. Daddy drops one of Mom's homemade buns in his plate of stew and it hits gravy like a bomb. Splatters everything. A carrot whizzes past Robbie's ear like a piece of shrapnel. Mom frowns.

'Smooth move, Exlax,' I say, just to let them know I'm not completely lost to them.


TO RECAP. Grampy's gone. Nature's coming apart at the seams and all the stuffing's flying out. Bambi's true self has been exposed (disgusting carnivore). The Comet continues to give Daddy, though not me, 'small car ease and handling, fuel economy and simplicity of maintenance and repair.' On the personal front, I have failed biology and do I care? I know where all the essential parts are and what to do with them. Not that I'll be doing anything with mine. I'm thinking about switching religions, perhaps becoming an Altheist [*sick*]. I'm prepared to accept Buck's invitation to sing at the Lantern, *if* he calls in time and begs my forgiveness.

In the meantime, I talked Robbie into phoning Trudy, impersonating Buck ('duuuuh'), and cancelling *her* date to sing. *Say Trude, now that I think of it, you can't carry a tune worth squat.* Something like that.

When she answered, Robbie got a fit of the giggles, and said, 'Here's Marsha.'

'Oh, hi, Trudy,' I said gaily (hope you gag on a swizzle stick). 'Just calling to wish you luck' (hope it slashes your vocal cords).

In summary, I'd have to say that I'm pretty much tarred in my own black thoughts and don't expect I'll live to see the New Year.

I RESOLVE to dissolve.

NEW YEAR'S EVE. Yours truly is all dressed to go. Really go, if you know what I mean. I've got on my black dress, black nether wear, and a corsage I bought for myself that's gone kind of brown, kind of rotten, on account of having to keep it in my room. Looks like compost pinned to my chest. Ah yes, organic matter, like myself. This getup, my going-away outfit, is cleverly concealed beneath my housecoat. Don't want the folks to suspect anything's up. While they're watching Guy Lombardo on TV and shoving popcorn into their faces, I'll be on Highway 22, bride of the white line, marrying some transport truck. Me, done to a turn on the grill.

Robbie's spent most of the day rubbing balloons on his head and sticking them to the wall. His hair stands straight out, alive with static, as he works himself to a lather playing an invisible guitar, in the throes of a soundless yet demented version of 'The Night Has a Thousand Eyes.' I'll miss him. But not much.

I take a last fond look at the folks. Good hearts all in all, and to prove it, Daddy reaches into his pants pocket, pulls out the keys to the Comet and tosses them over to me.

He WINKS, and says, 'Why don't you go to that dance at the Lantern, Princess. Show them what you're made of. Get up on that stage and sing. Sit around waitin' for people to ask, you'll never get anywhere in life.'

'Now, Daddy,' says Mom.

'Now, Mom,' says Daddy.

'_____,' they both say, when I whip off my housecoat and stand before them, transformed, reborn, ready to party.

IT'S NO NIGHT for hair, believe me. As I traipse giddily out the door, the wind grabs my fancy French twist like the knob on a joystick and yanks it viciously around my head. Do I look prettily tousled by the time I get in the car? No, more like a hag recently exhumed. Never mind. I'm driving down the road, getting somewhere in life. *Dooo whaa, dooo whaa ditty.* It feels *sooo* good to have my hands on the wheel. In control. Though I've got butterflies the size of bats in my stomach. And the wind's gone positively mental. I can feel it frisking the car, sucking at the tires and trying to draw it into the ditch. A mad dog with the road in its teeth.

Over the top of McLeod's Hill and down, at the junction of Draper and Hardbargain Road, is the Lantern, sitting pretty as a Christmas ornament.

I *zoom* down that hill and kind of lift off the ground, like the wind's snatched the road out from under me. *Teeeee, heeeee,* I hear Grampy laugh in my ear. And I realize then, approaching the Lantern at a truly wicked speed, that I'm about to crash this party in style. That I'm going to pop through that wall there like a woman jumping out of a cake. And I do. I close my eyes tight, then hear this metal-wrenching wood-splitting glass-shattering explosion, and when I open them again, guess what, I'm in.

I drive through a shrieking diving confusion of people, clawing to get out of my way – all couples I know (I wave) – and park in front of the stage. *Parallel* park too. I've never pulled that one *off* before, and I'm tickled pink.

First, I check to see if there are any unseemly organs hanging out of my body (I don't suppose this is what Daddy meant when he said to show them what I'm made of). Everything is ship-shape, so I get out of the car. No problem, as the door seems to be missing. I brush a swatch of the colour-keyed vinyl roof off my shoulder, then hop lightly onto the stage.

I notice that Trudy's mouth is frozen into a round red 'o' of astonishment. She brays once then faints, hitting the deck like a slaughtered animal.

Two strings on Buck's guitar are broken and wildly probing the air like antennae. He stands there shaking his head (admiringly? is that a gleam in his eye?).

The wind that raced me into the Lantern, a close second, is now wearing about sixteen party hats and having a riot lifting girls' dresses.

I step over Trudy, take my place at the mike, and suddenly, you want transportation, I'm singing.

# India

MAY, MINNIE, MAUD for God's sake, or Myrna – even worse. Names she might have worn like a crown of link sausages. But no, it was not to be. Her mother opened her eyes in heaven during the birth and saw two archangels walking hand in hand. She named her baby girl Michael Gabriel, stifling the protest of the paternal great-aunts (May, Minnie, Maud, and Myrna) by saying, 'You have not seen what I have seen.'

The great-aunts were relentless in their disapproval. The Island was home to neither snakes nor Catholics, and they disliked sinuous fanciful names, names that suggested the impossible. One honest name, chosen from within the family, was all anyone needed. But their nephew's son, who worked on the boats, had married off the Island into a family nobody knew anything about. This was the result: a girl child named Michael Gabriel.

Their names clanging in the air like school bells, that's what most of the Island children heard when they were called in to supper. They heard their names ringing and they raced each other like dogs down the street, home to hot kitchens, steaming bowls of mashed potatoes, and platters of burnt-black meat. When Michael Gabriel's mother called her in, a dark deck of ancestors standing behind her on the porch, the name travelled like a charm through the mute evening air. Michael Gabriel, playing alone by the dock or in the woods, picked up the lilting thread and followed it, a long poem winding through the dusk.

Though Michael Gabriel's mother never talked much about her dispersed and wandering family, she sought them in her mind and addressed them privately. Now and then she heard back from one of them. A postcard might arrive from anywhere in the world, the message indecipherable (or so they complained at the Island post office), yet clear enough to Michael Gabriel's mother who would close her eyes and grip the card tightly in her hands. Sometimes presents were sent, crazy presents in the aunts' opinion: painted eggs, a scapular from Rome kissed by the Pope; a large red smiling Buddha that resembled some of the Island uncles; a sistrum; silk robes; games with instructions in Arabic or Greek; drums; flutes made of bone; and Day-of-the-Dead confections which featured marzipan skeletons rising out of shortbread coffins. Sometimes one of these mysterious relations even turned up in person. They always arrived without warning and stood quietly at the screen door staring in.

When Michael Gabriel's teacher caught her daydreaming he tried to snap her name. He tried to grind it through his teeth and reduce it to dust. 'Michael Gabriel' was the sweetest sound he ever made. The great-aunts were filled to the skin with their names, like cans of stew. Not her. Her name was mercurial, slipped out of her body like a soul, became a hovering dragonfly or an alcove whose boundary expanded whenever she reached out to touch it. Her name was all the bright objects in the sky bursting like fireworks around her. 'Michael Gabriel' ... the teacher said it so beautifully that tears came to his eyes. Hearing her name she'd glance up and the rest of the class would turn to her and squint as though she were pure unshaded light.

She was popular but hard to get at. Burrowing children with moth-soft hair and hands fought to be near her and couldn't find the way. Her name was a little door that didn't open. She was invited to parties and won all the prizes; asked to play games and undermined them, enlarging or unravelling them until they made no sense. She told stories about hell that came to her out of the ground under the rocks, and gave the children nightmares that neither daylight nor the warm breath of parents could melt.

People complained, but what could her mother do? She had chosen from among the angels, not the aunts. The angels wore white, or nothing at all; the aunts favoured maroon, ugly plaids, and brooches made of cheap coloured glass. Whenever Michael Gabriel came to visit them, the front windows of the old family home darkened as they stood watching her run up the lane with a bouquet of leaves. One of them would reluctantly accept the gift, which disappeared instantly from sight, while the others hugged her, scratched her with their brooches, and offered powdered bulldog cheeks to be kissed. Michael Gabriel kissed them carefully, unlike her Island cousins whose wet lips plopped kisses like spitballs. The cousins tumbled in trailing mud and burrs, scuffed up the hardwood floors, left fish hooks stuck in the sofa, occasionally a dried worm or a dead frog on the tea table. For the great-aunts they emptied their pockets and their heads, showing their new-found treasures and telling everything that had happened since their last visit. Michael Gabriel's secrets were discreetly wrapped and well hidden. She left her small white shoes at the door, met each crabby question politely, and possessed the room like an adult. Her manner irritated the aunts. Should she clear her throat musically and ask after their health, their caterpillar-thick eyebrows twitched with irritation. If she said, I beg your pardon, instead of *whaat*, teacups hit saucers with a noisy clatter. Unlike her cousins, she wasn't given to fart jokes or loud barking burps. The great-aunts, understanding as they did the true fabric of the family, developed a belief that she was not one of them at all, but a foundling, fool's gold dropped in their nest by idle hand-holding angels.

When Michael Gabriel was five she found him sleeping on the green velvet couch. Night was dawdling into day, excitement just beginning to trickle through the branches of the trees. Colour had not yet crept back into things. Shadows curled around him like black cloth baring only the side of his face, shoulder, and thigh – pale as shell. She moved closer, smelled distance. She moved closer still, until she could feel his cool breath on her cheek. She saw then that he wasn't asleep, but had been watching her. 'Michael Gabriel,' he whispered. Her name rustled like silk in her ears. 'Michael Gabriel,' he whispered a little louder, and her name swept out of the room taking night, a child in hand, with it. Birds all round the house went wild with song.

Michael Gabriel's mother recited poetry, the only form of prayer she liked, and waltzed with her daughter across the cracked kitchen linoleum. She often stood at the window warming her hands in the sun and willing her eyes to see as far as the mainland. She was looking for herself over there, dancing *petits tours* and pirouettes all the way down the road to Mexico. She'd have binges of sadness and Michael Gabriel would have to stroke her back until her soul settled down and tucked itself in, like a cat on a cold day. Mornings she'd wake up fiercely disappointed in dreams full of rock and water and gulls that nattered like the great-aunts. She was accused of letting Michael Gabriel run wild. They didn't understand. She had learned years ago not to worry. If her baby rolled under the bed and spent a happy afternoon with the dust devils, or somehow got herself buried in the laundry basket – no matter. Powers far greater than her own were in control. This apparent lack of concern fed the great-aunts' suspicions about Michael Gabriel's legitimacy. They expected misfortune daily. But the girl, it seemed, was put on this earth to abuse their expectations. Childhood accidents eluded her however close she came to them. She frequently wandered into the lake over her head without drowning; safely set fire to numerous beds and bushes; and accepted candy from the seamiest of strangers who then failed to spirit her off to some unspeakable end.

Angels being what they are, Michael Gabriel grew up with an exaggerated sense of her own safety. The rough-and-tumble cousins saw death everywhere. Saw it rising on the lake, saw it falling with night out of the trees. It was sewn into their names and written in the blunt lines of their palms. They chased it with snares, shotguns, and crazy drunken rides down dirt roads. They chased it in the boathouse and the bush as they screwed their Susies and Bettys and Barbs. Michael Gabriel studied the beautifully etched lines on her palm and didn't see it there, hiding under those little woven vines of flesh. Her name might lose its lustre, or settle into a shape that could drive her mad. The black bird that carries it in her beak might let it fall to the ground. She didn't know.

His name was Jules. He had pushed through the screen door one morning and surprised them. Her mother hugged him hard, like a lost doll, and cried until her loneliness let go. By this time Michael Gabriel was fifteen and her Island cousins were trying to stick their fat tongues in her mouth every chance they got. The tongue, Jules told her, is a dancer. But the tongues of the cousins were thick and tough. A certain walk, a stiff swagger brutalizing motion, a certain way of moving the tongue, against language. They pounded words with their tongues the way they pounded the heads of fish with rocks. 'Howz Jewlz,' they sneered when they saw him in town. 'Hey, howzit goin' ... Je*w*lz.' He'd stare at them indifferently as though they were cows, then pass by, moving fluidly along each bend and curve of the path. When he looked at them like that a fist tightened in their chests. They hated him. Him with his white skin and green eyes. 'Fag.' Spit snapped against the rocks just right – 'gobbed good' – but they weren't satisfied. Something about him they couldn't see that the women did. Their girl-friends watched him like prey, forgot everything else. Even the great-aunts had started wearing rouge, a girlish pink, then more feverish shades of red. 'Piss,' the cousins said, and fresh spit gleamed on the rocks. He knew something they didn't. Which was true. He *knew* how to use his tongue.

Michael Gabriel's mother put on her party dress and stayed up late. During the night smoke rings drifted whole into Michael Gabriel's room on a steady undercurrent of talk and laughter. Her mother slept peacefully deep into the afternoon and woke with the sun soft, poised above the bay, ready to slip into an envelope of water and be delivered to the underworld. When she got up, Jules made her coffee and fried-egg sandwiches, the yolk runny the way she liked it. The three of them sat on the porch in the twilight, feet up on the railing, listening to the water sing. It purled around the dock telling them the whereabouts underwater of sinkers, bottles, snagged lures, and sunfish. Michael Gabriel's mother licked a dribble of yolk from between her fingers and smiled. The water switched from the Mills Brothers to Handel. This was heaven.

While Jules was on the Island, the angels might have heard a hissing noise coming from there, like a kettle boiling in a distant room. It was talk. Whisperings carried from ear to ear until the whole place was squirming with sound. They would have heard what Jules and Michael Gabriel were doing every afternoon on the green velvet couch while her mother slept. The great-aunts, formidable virgins themselves, could describe these goings-on in detail. People started dropping in for tea. They ate up the stale store-bought cookies, smacking their lips, and eyed the green couch lewdly. One or two even dared to slip over to it, feel the velvet, and raise the toss pillows, hands trembling, as though expecting to find rattlers coiled underneath.

Michael Gabriel enjoyed the gossip. She liked the way their names entwined and multiplied. Their echoing names followed them everywhere. Like a procession of bodyguards, or a stream of altar boys. They walked into the woods and their names embraced them in the dark. But when Jules suddenly left, was suddenly gone without word or warning, and the merry-go-round of talk wound slowly down and died, her name flattened like a good solid skipping stone and settled in her hand. She knew that if she was careless and tossed it across the water after him, it would no longer return to her. She sat down to consider, sinking into the green velvet couch as into a soft shadowy deafness.

The great-aunts heaved a sigh of relief. The cousins got together and bought her a pot of mums. Her father came home from working on the boats and wanted to know his daughter's name. 'India,' her mother said musing, taken with the sound, drifting past him at the door. And the fluffy, cherubic clouds that had hung so long over the Island, like decorations in a play, were reeled up far into the sky.

# Patronage

THE GODS get by on charm, that's their secret. It's the black greased-back hair, the flashing smile that momentarily sears the eyes, the sex lights in their cars that draw us in. Swordfish cufflinks and satin underwear. Salty, whispering lips. The gods glide into our hearts point blank. Slip presents into our open hands. Gifts. *El rewardo,* as your father used to say. Do you remember our life together? It was a peak time, madness unfurling, and your father buzzing around the edge of it like a filthy little fly. For two years he drove everyone crazy speaking Spanish. His Spanish. *El batso,* he would say, *el nutso.* He stole tips off restaurant tables. He liked to tell how he knocked your mother up, banged her against a brick wall behind the Majestic Theatre. They laughed about it at Sunday dinner, your older sister choking on the ham while he demonstrated how her head was flatter than yours. Embarrassment was a kind of currency in your family. When you were a boy your father used to grab you and pull down your pants in front of guests. For a joke. What a nut, they laughed. A pair of nuts, he corrected. *El nutso.* Your father was like a body falling in another room.

Everyone was writing rat poetry then. I wrote a poem in which the rats had red lips and were the lithe blue princes of the bay. The bay was my bay. The body of water I carried around with me and laid down like a placemat wherever I needed it. At night I set it in front of my downtown apartment, my little sea shell slum. With cockroaches running inside the walls along the wiring like a network of familiars, I submerged the heart of the city. Cars rolled into waves that rocked me to sleep. Currents carried drunks and midnight walkers away, their anguished dead-of-night prayers floating ahead of them like black dogs. As I slept, I stocked my bay with drop-offs into darkness and lithe blue Speedo rats with red lips and southern tongues.

This bed of memories is a decaying fertile mulch. I poke

around in it and I see your mother coming to visit, trying to comprehend the attraction of dirt fossilized in corners and baggy second-hand clothes. Dents in the wall where people have thrown things at one another, where heads have hit cracking plaster. She braved the stairs and the treacherous winding walk across the roof, and was smiling in at me through the ripped screen when the floor boards gave way beneath her feet. Amazing that they should ripen into perfect rottenness the moment she stepped on them, light as a moth in her white Amalfi shoes. This is what marriage into your father's family must have been like. Shadows cruising a bloodline for centuries then suddenly appearing, like a bruise, all around her. Those times your father intruded, blundering stupidly over the threshold, bullying us with the wrong kind of passion – and *he* never sank through the floor. Rottenness upheld him. But your mother married into misfortune, didn't she, the ground always shifting beneath her feet. At their wedding, all those sleazy uncles of yours stalking the bridesmaids, introducing chaos. Your mother was the pretty one, dressed in silk, smiling, hopeful, disappearing in a cloud of dust.

Your feet never seemed to touch the ground. Not for long anyway. After I moved in, you moved out. You got lost for a while, then came back and found a place around the corner, the landlord a weasel with inflamed eyes. Just the sort of person you like. You decided to become an actor, and then a teacher. Then a mirage. You slid into basement bars with the scum, drove taxi for a time, washed dishes. Got a job in a local radio station and flew to Montreal to buy a pair of sunglasses. Once you went out to dinner with friends and called me at three in the morning, from Baltimore, asking for money to pay the bill. You were a target that never stopped moving. I watched you ebbing in and out of the city, bursting through doors, rushing down stairs. That shirt I gave you for your birthday, the one with the lobsters on it. Well, all I ever saw was the back of it, claws frozen in a parting gesture. When you weren't here there was no one to feed the fiction. Your mistake. It was your myth, remember. Not mine.

Sometimes, in dreams, you surface. You loom out of a depth, dolphin-smooth and powerful, secrets in your eyes. You might give me something, tell me something. Instead, you flip yourself like a large silver moon and land, bright side turned away, like a stranger.

When you met me I still climbed trees, I didn't know how to act in the city. I liked running, real running, gut-busting, erratic with dodges and the smell of escape. I had animal blood in me. I was wild and rough like a storm in the bay. Everything in the city looked pissed on – claimed by someone or something else. I kept to myself. You discovered me like a spider under a rock, a coiled snake. You introduced me to your friends, whose tongues fluttered like leaves, and to your father, who said I had big feet. A country girl with all that fierce innocence clenched in two rock-hard fists. Now I'm amber-coloured, uncoiled, down from the trees.

You accepted gifts like tribute. I have this image of the sea and this image of you. People walking down a green hill, stepping onto the burning sand. People trusted you, instinctively. Believed in you. When I think of you I have this image of people standing before the rocking sea, their arms full. Something about you larger than I can say. There were presents from people who hardly knew you. Money and food. Bottles of good wine. Children on the street handed you their treasures, their lunch plums and stones still pocket-warm and glowing with luck. Your friends agonized over the right gifts for you; expensive, special, meaningful gifts with the intensity of their love buried in them. They never seemed to realize that you gave their presents away, and only thought what a wonderful coincidence it was if you forgot and gave their own present back to them. I couldn't believe the hands extended to you. Strange offerings too, witchy things, knots of hair, paws and tails, talismans, and pieces of glass that were tiny windows to who knows what weird sights. Valued possessions were orphaned on your doorstep. (Once, a jar of pickled bees.) You received unexpected invitations from priests scribbled on holy cards. Life stories from almost everyone, confessions and broken hearts, a jerky stream of unhappiness poured into your hands. I remember this smarmy guy stopping you on the street one day and handing you his shoes. 'For you,' he said. Black pointy shoes with clickers on the heels, sweaty and foul inside. He started taking off his pants too, but you stopped him, your fingers touching his wrist. For a time after that I could hear you wherever you went. Clickety-click, on the street turning the corner, smart-ass walking, standing at the door with that grin of yours – what I wouldn't give you. Then afterwards, clickety-click, duck tail down the stairs. Gone. Blue ravenous sea and golden light, all your gifts intact.

And yet you were never free. Your father just kept reeling you in. You weren't as different as you supposed; and there were ties, of course, and loyalty. Do you recall that family picnic, your cousins screaming with your father after them, pecker bouncing like a dog's, cheeks surprisingly firm. He drank too much, yelled too much. Stormed out of the house brandishing the bread knife like a warrior. Your parents' neighbours were used to suburban violence muffled by huge ball-shaped shrubs, but couldn't get used to the sight of a man lying in the middle of the road in broad daylight, sobbing. He didn't like confinement, your father. Remember how he smashed his head and hands through a wall of glass to touch you? He conned you with his blood. Your blood. It made the same black stain on the ground.

I haven't mentioned crows, have I?

That time you came home from the north, from some expedition or other with an archaeologist friend. It was hot in the city, the way it gets here, the air hypnotic, pressing in, heavy as an illness. Rain, unfulfilled promise. I lay awake most of the night staring through folds in the darkness and got up early. My mind was clear. You were coming, the planet was tilted in my direction. The morning was still as breath held and the sun bulged red over the buildings while the birds, guiding it, sang their urgent dissolving story. I pushed through the screen door and walked out back carrying a box of old party dresses that I'd bought at a flea market a few days before. I lifted them out carefully, organdies and muslins deeply fragrant with perfume and must, and began tying them however I could, by straps and sashes, around the branches of the tree that arched over the roof. Some were delicate and airy, others boisterously polka-dotted, or slinky, gaudy as parrots. One of them, densely crinolined and glinting with sequins – worn to a dance it would have rubbed a partner's hands raw – bristled stiffly on its branch like an aggressive pink star. I hung them all up then sat down and waited. I let my eyes take a spider-walk down cracks and minute paths getting lost for a while in smaller erosions and the cunning creeping politics of rooftop weeds.

About midday a slight breeze slipped into the city and came hissing around the roof, lured to the tree. The dresses shivered and rustled, as if waking from a long sleep. A French lace sleeve lifted – and dropped. A satin skirt billowed for a moment, then abruptly collapsed. The breeze picked at the dresses in a desultory way, tried on one or two, did a slow pirouette in a gorgeous canary-yellow gown, then slipped over the roof, attracted by a squall of red-haired boys skirmishing in the alley below. A keener, more vigorous wind followed, possessing the tree like a demon. One touch and the dresses whirled and leapt, bodied out, substantial as goddesses. This is what you saw standing at the top of the stairs.

And you came down to me, and brought your arms around me, and your body, cool as silk, dressed mine. And something else. You brought the rain.

I don't know why I started this. Something to do, I guess. It's a bad habit, straining my eyes backward, whites only directed at the future. I think I wore my face out, laughing. You were very funny. And crying. Sometimes you weren't. So funny. We were charmed, you said, full of the same quirky light. Blessed. But I'm forgetting: I was the ruthless one. I conjured you and you had to come. I took what you gave me and then stopped believing. I lost faith and you dematerialized. Though I could find you again, if I wanted to. Couldn't I? All I'd have to do is look for trouble. I know you're out there endearing yourself to some difficulty.

Swimming with sharks, running with rats. You're the aberration, the disturbance in the distance. Like static on the shortwave, like sin. I didn't realize then that some things don't break, no matter what you do to them, no matter how they're tortured. So many comings and goings. Doors slammed and tires squealing. Who was it? Which of us was left behind the last time to eat dust? I forget. Isn't that funny. It doesn't matter now, though, does it? Because it's finished. *El finito,* as your father used to say. Over and over. *Ad nauseam.*

# Man with the Axe

ONE SPRING Hooligan came home with a wooden leg in his mouth. Erie had been listening all that week to thaw, a trickle of melt tickling her inner ear, the sound of water dripping off the eaves, *drip* into that handful of bare stones by the corner of the barn, *drop* off the branches of the forsythia out front. Like tears, she thought, cold tears. Then reconsidered, what with the lake opening up and boats arriving from the mainland carrying news and visitors. Tears of joy, or relief. No, that wasn't right either, and she did like to get things right, finding the exact place that words met events. She had literary ambitions, though not openly nurtured. The evidence was buried in her bureau drawer, well hidden below several layers of underwear. The everyday woollies on top, summer cottons below, next a thin layer of silk surprising to the delving hand as a cold current snaking through shallow water. The silks had belonged to Erie's Aunt Elaine, who had lived for a time in France.

In family lore Elaine was the restless one, the one with *ants in her pants.* She twitched and itched, unsettled as a wild bird on a bobbing branch. In pictures she was the disruptive blur, the streak of light cutting through their tight embrace. No one could hold her. *I'm not marrying this rock pile,* she said at eighteen, and left. She wrote home occasionally – short, energetic messages, the words themselves seeming to sprint and tumble like acrobats off the page. Slow suspicious readers, the family had trouble catching even these. They thought her aimlessly adrift, or saw her wantonly snagged in the silken sly arms of foreigners, when what she clearly needed was the honest anchoring touch of an island man. *She'll die young,* predicted Aunt Velma, who had always been jealous of Elaine. But Elaine was too elusive and early death fell like a sudden obliterating snow on Velma instead. Planted by the kitchen sink, a slab of cake in hand and a lump of lard clogging her arteries, damming her heart, she was a target;

what could death do but knock her flat like a disgruntled and abusive husband? So it was Velma who failed to see forty while Elaine's life flowed on, finally pooling in a small package that Erie one day pulled out of the mailbox.

She unwrapped it reverently, thinking it might contain ashes, or Elaine's delicate bird bones. She certainly hadn't expected to find underwear, *lingerie* rather, slippery and spirited as Elaine herself. It practically leapt out of the box, splashing up against Erling who had just come in from the barn. He caught at the flying rat's nest of silk, a shock like fine cold skin pouring into his hands, and dropped it, horrified. Only once before had he touched anything like it, Manny Nearing's bare bum in 1909, and that too had been an accident. He shot Erie a look, a sharp fan of annoyance that flared open and trembled ominously for a moment before snapping shut.

*Don't goggle your frog eyes at me,* she said in a low growl, stooping to retrieve the pearly soft tangle – almost weightless, like gathering vapour into her arms – and he was gone. The screen door slapped shut and he marched across the yard, ducking back into the barn, where Tidy and Maureen's hefty brown rumps were scarcely distinguishable in the warm gloom.

Erie had to get rid of their aunt's bequest (or remains, how was one to view it?) before Erling returned for lunch. Unmentionables, indeed. Apparently some things weren't fit for words. She tried to picture him, bread and beef stew wadded in one cheek, making a joke of it, this sensual assault. Hardly. He'd forcibly forget the incident; in his mind tamp it down like a freshly buried thing. Over the years they had established a common ground for conversation and you wouldn't dare ruck that up with inventive or silly talk. *Would you,* Erie remembers asking herself as she laid Elaine's gift in her bureau, giving it a place among the hidden inventory of the house. A proper cover somehow for her writing, the broken bits of stories, the letters addressed to no one in particular, the shy stuttering beginnings of a novel. Her soul stretched out in longhand and scattered on loose sheets of paper. She wrote secretly at night while Erling slept. *Moonlighting* she liked to think. Furtive, shadow-sifting work done by lantern or candle light, even soft slanting moonlight itself. Ghostly sources of illumination that could lead her anywhere while her brother lay snoring and dreamless in the dark back bedroom.

Of course Erie didn't try to fool herself. She understood that Erling was the real writer in the family. Every Sunday after church he composed his weekly column for their local paper, *The Gossip*. Euchre parties, dances, weddings and births, bake sales, visits paid and repaid – he presided over social commerce in the community like a finicky omniscient author. Unlike the correspondent from Silverwater who padded her column with prayers, poems and gardening tips, Erling crafted a solid substantial block of Blue Lake news, a densely crowded mirror in which anyone could look and see themselves swinging a bat, singing at the Glee Club, or chatting with their cousin Molly at the Come and Go Tea. He didn't have to scrounge for it, either. News came to him steadily like a wind trained to heel. Wasn't the phone always ringing or someone dropping by? People loved to bend his ear, to fill it with those tids and tads that by the end of the week added up to a full page report. He'd tinker the whole afternoon, working like a kid on the engine of an old car. He wasn't satisfied until it purred like a cat; a contented, well-fed, benign creature. That was how he presented their island life. The same smiling character dressed in slightly different detail from one week to the next. He doctored unpleasant news, delivered it with pastoral care. Erling concentrated on a specific kind of weather that was man-made and unfailingly clement. No wonder he didn't hear the thief in the ice that Erie heard. All that week her ear itched with a telltale trickle of melt like a tap dripping somewhere, and soon water speaking in a hundred, then a thousand voices through rocks and trees and shifting earth. Distracting, listening to winter weep itself away like that. By the time Erling took notice and announced to the world, *Well, folks, spring has sprung,* an unfurling pouncing vernal light had overwhelmed them all. Strangely unexpected, like Hooligan bounding across the yard and skidding to a stop in front of Erie, a wooden leg in his mouth and a sliver of mischief buried deep in his one good eye.

HOOLIGAN was a real presence in any room. Rock-solid and black as pitch. He had a snake of a tail, fat as an arm and powerful. You got your knees and other low-lying objects out of range when he was happy or excited. Of note among his accomplishments: a short ecclesiastical career (he'd once been owned by a priest); progeny stretching from one end of the island to the other; and murder, quarry all harried to death.

His origins were as dark as he was. He might have wandered off one of the reserves, or swum across the channel from the mainland. Who knows? No one could recall Hooligan as a pup. He appeared full grown and half-blind, having left one of his eyes like a surveillance device in some former life.

Some dogs you can ignore. Shut the door in their beseeching faces and they eventually grow restless and move on. Not Hooligan. When he first came sniffing around the farm, he liked the place and decided right then to stay. He sat on their doorstep the better part of three days, affably tenacious as a salesman, until Erie finally relented and let him in. An irreversible invitation, she realized, like letting a child into your house. Though you couldn't really compare Hooligan to any child. He'd ripped up his innocence like a rag long ago. He was full of tricks. He could get his nose up a skirt faster than the practised hand of a lover. Something about a woman's startled scream gave him the shivers. He enjoyed a good show of emotion, especially in its extreme forms. You could tell he'd been a priest's dog. He would put his paw in your hand, stare encouragingly, coercively – his one eye focused on you like a pistol – and you'd confess anything to him. Erie had. He knew everything she knew about the boy who courted her for two years before marrying the lake.

His name was Jimmy Brooke. Every Saturday night he rode his bike over from Sheg to see her. He was garrulous and generous, spilling like light into the yard. She'd race down the stairs to greet him, a good-looking boy, with a gorgeous head of hair, thick as tuft of grass. They used to go dancing in town, or on hot nights steal down to the lake for a swim. He stripped easily – he wasn't shy – and she lost time watching him. Male hands and faces were all she'd ever seen before, and even those were often turned against a woman's looking. He was easy in the water. He opened the lake with a high smooth dive. Once in he moved languidly, admiring her on the shore, so transparently eager to be with him she'd be tearing at the buttons of her dress.

For one so talkative, he went without a whisper. By the time she was ready to join him that night he had already disappeared. She stood gripping and wringing her clothing, waiting for the joke to end, for him to break the surface with a laugh. Unbearable, the peacefulness of the lake, a terrible tormenting calm.

To Hooligan, she cursed her slowness. She might have saved him, or followed him. Hooligan was well acquainted with the possibilities, and, with at least mock-sorrow, would place his head in her lap and sigh loudly.

Sure he knew a few things about them, their hoarded secrets, fusty and dry as longdead mice. Small change really, compared to some lives. Erie said as much, what was there to know? After Mother and then Father died, she and Erling had settled down with each other contentedly enough. Working the farm, meals together, small talk, as good as married except for the sex part of it, and she supposed some brothers and sisters worked that one out to their satisfaction as well. Oh, you couldn't write *that* in your local paper, but you could tell a dog like Hooligan who loved to scrabble in the dirt.

Shameless creatures, dogs. Shit-sniffers and disturbers. Behind a show of obedience they follow their own rules, and their own etiquette, which seems to consist of private acts performed in public. Dogs take pleasure in unsettling things, digging up and dragging into sight what would best stay below ground and forgotten. Like Hooligan dropping that leg at Erie's feet, then gazing up at her eagerly, ingenuously.

As she picked it up, it pricked her imagination. Comfortable in her palm, snug as a rolling pin or a baseball bat, it made her

wonder. Relics. Everyone had them, a wristbone in the silverware, a skull hanging on a nail in the shed. People thieved like
crows when it came to that sort of thing, skeletons found in
caves. It happened on the island. Bones wandered away in hip
pockets and purses before the museum folks could get anywhere
near them. She appreciated the fascination with something that
had survived death, that glowed moon-white, so smooth to touch
you felt capable of stroking the unknown right out of it. At least
Jim was safe from looting. Or was he? Erie habitually thought of
him as he had once been, but a lover of the water now, held and
rocked by mothering currents. Though for all she knew, he
might have slipped out of his skin and shattered on a reef like a
dish hitting a rock. He might have been carried in countless
directions, washing up on shore, spangling the island like a broken bone necklace. Even now re-entering her life in some
unforeseeable way, borne in a bird's beak, a stranger's hand.

A wooden leg wasn't a bone naturally, though it served.
Someone must have been attached to it at one time, a husband or
a sweetheart. A pirate, God knows. How did a person lose such a
thing, anyway? Easy enough, Erie supposed. You get involved in
a barroom brawl. Some tough gets his hands on it, then uses it
like a pestle to pulverize glass and flesh.

No, rather this: You've been chopping trees, hewing beams all
morning for the new house, and you're exhausted. You find
some shade and wolf down lunch. The leg chafes a bit so you
loosen it. Settling back, you drift into a troubled sleep, then wake
with a start. Just in time to see a large black dog vanish into the
bush, jaws clamped firmly – teeth like nails – on the hard flesh of
a wooden leg, yours.

THE MOMENT the phone rang, one long and a short, Erie knew
that someone had picked up the scent. It didn't take long in a
place as small as Blue Lake for word to get around. Genuine
news – not the old stuff Erling dished out – spread infectiously
from mind to mind, enjoying a short feverish existence before

turning belly-up into history. Erling was simply the one who gave it last rites before burying it in his column.

Nola Wilks' voice buzzed in her ear like a bee in a blossom. 'You know, Erie, your dog came ripping out of the bush behind our place carrying something, I couldn't tell what exactly, though it looked like oak to me by the grain. I imagine he's been home with it by now, has he?'

'Yes, he's back.'

'Well, this might sound kind of funny, but like I said to Bun, that's no hunk of lumber Hooligan's got there ... looked like a *pegleg* to me.'

'Why, that's exactly what it is, Nola.'

'*Go on*, really? Who could it belong to, I wonder? No one from around here, that's for sure. Maybe some sailor off one of the boats. What's it look like, Erie, is there anything on it?'

'You mean, like a sock?'

'No, no, marks, scratches, a bear might have, well, you know. Any moss on it, it might've been in the bush a long time.'

'Hooligan's had a bit of a chew. Beyond that I'd say this leg's in pretty good shape.'

'Hmph, smells fishy to me. Bet there's more to this than meets the eye. It's kind of creepy, if you know what I mean. I'm telling you, Erie, a body hardly feels safe any more.'

Erie paused to consider the safety of Nola's body, which was in fact invulnerable, calling up comparisons to heavy machinery, though she took in the suggestion of danger, nonetheless. Two women talking, that's all it took to spark a birth, a genesis, to entice someone out of the shadows. A lurking presence, someone just waiting to try that leg on, take a few tottering steps, then wheel through the door whole as any man.

TROUBLE WAS, spring made everyone a bit tipsy and unsteady on their feet. Who could walk a straight line with dandelions popping like burning suns out of an earth that was shaking with life? Minds and tongues quickened, hands speeded up and grew expressive, swooping and carving, trying to define and encompass the thing. The thing being, in most cases, the identity of the man with the wooden leg.

Consensus took on a life of its own, metamorphic and unpredictable. One minute he was a cranky and miserly old trapper who lost his life in the bush, the next he was younger, lithe and cunning, a drifter who had been seen about town hanging out with a bad crowd.

He'd been noticed, no doubt about it. In the Ocean House that one leg *tap tapping* on the hardwood floor made William Porter glance up from the guest book. What Bill saw, against a dazzling background of white light flooding through the French doors, was the kind of person he discouraged from staying at his hotel. Not that this man was a tramp or anything, far from it. He was faultlessly groomed, and his clothing an expensive cut, if a bit out of date. No, it was something else about him, that slight scar above his lip, perhaps some immaterial detail, that told Bill he was a gambler. That he would fleece Bill's customers playing acey deucy and one-eyed jacks, simple games but effective as leeches in sucking rich veins dry. Then one night he'd skip town, leaving nothing behind but a haze of stale smoke.

*Sorry,* Bill raised his hands helplessly, *no room, we're all booked up.* A lie that drew poison like a poultice. The stranger narrowed his eyes, moved closer, breath cool as fog. Bill froze. Blood rushed from his hands and squeezed his heart. Fear blundered out of him, and the man laughed. Then turned, pivoting on his bad leg, he walked back toward the French doors, but slowly, dissolving in light, *tap tapping* on the hardwood so that the sound of it, the rhythm stayed with Bill and he remembered. He'd never forget, he said.

Memory served William Porter well, as it served everyone, presenting facts of a shifting and malleable property, fluid enough to pour into any mold. The man with the wooden leg was painstakingly, if playfully, restored.

As far as Erie was concerned, the leg might have been a tossed bone that any flop-eared mutt could gnaw on. It seemed all you had to do was shake the dumb inanimate thing until it sprouted limbs. *She* could conjure a man out of it and do a better job than the good Lord Himself, though that wasn't the point, she realized. The man's true identity didn't really matter; he was selfless and sacrificial. They killed him off repeatedly, speculating on this death or that, then brought him back in a flood of words. Resurrected and sustained him in talk. And how he had multiplied. He was an army, a forest of men by the time Erling got in there and started hacking away, working steadily, methodically, in the end finishing him off with a couple of resounding *whacks.*

He dropped a few well-placed hints here and there, then finally came out with it. He ran a story one week about a man on the west end, a carpenter, who had by some crazy mistake received a whole crate of wooden legs from the States. He'd been using them up as best he could, Erling reported, as railings and table legs, but still had a pile of them in the shed, and *yes* he had noticed a black dog, *a brute of a thing,* snooping around his place awhile back....

Entirely plausible, Erie thought when she read Erling's account in the paper. Why had a sane explanation not occurred to anyone else? This virgin-pale piece of wood they'd been dreaming on held as much interest as a fence post, a lifeless stump. Erling helped them see this in the sharper, unclotted light his prose provided. Reason had an edge and now they could use it to cut back all that nonsense about a mysterious stranger. How like her brother. Given a chance, he'd kill anything with common sense. As a boy, his plodding devotion to literal truth had made playing games with him almost impossible. Any flight of fancy, *let's pretend we're horses, let's gallop away,* would drive a stiff wedge of disapproval into his face. Erling held himself back like land that never touched water. *That's stupid,* he'd say, or primly, *Don't be childish.*

WELL, Hooligan wasn't the one who dropped it in the fire,

though he was lying on the hearth rug with his eye cocked open, when Erling did. *A cold night,* Erling muttered, unnerved by what he thought was the dog's amused stare.

Entering the room, Erie was startled to see the leg alive again and angling for their attention once more. Surely it was showing off, shooting blue flames, exhaling plumes of smoke and belching sparks. She sat down before it, compelled to watch it burn, letting it lure her and draw her in.

When Erling at last went up to bed, she found a stray sheet of paper in his desk, and in the splashing wavering firelight, with Hooligan half-asleep at her feet, she began to write. She had no idea what at first. She let her mind drift, phrases rising in waves. Then she saw something, someone, just the tip of a bobbing head, features uncertain. Her words, she knew, would have to be quick and strong as hands to grab that lilting silken hair and lift him out.

# *Unfinished*

LIKE A DREAM in the middle of the day. Like holding a river, holding moonlight, falling like mercury. Like remembering pain, inexactly. Like what is left. Like nothing.

I could send a fleet of searching metaphors and never find you. You have disappeared into one of those mythical cities, underwater, in the sky, whose doors don't open to people with hearts still clanging like tin pans in their chests. I am a bounty hunter with one instruction: *bring him back alive.*

A beginning, a middle, and an end. But your story wasn't finished, the plot was still unfolding, and now you're lying in it. What does that make you? Post-modern? Or simply, post-everything?

I remember standing at the window looking at the cedars out back, vaguely worrying, their foliage had grown so thin, lacy, I could see right through them to the children playing on the other side, swooping around the yard wearing sheets, doing crow imitations, *caw caw cawing* into the wind, until the real thing drifted in, black and silent, and settled ominously near, which stopped them dead in their tracks.

*Dogwatches.* You figure it out. And while you're at it, tell me what you do all day, or night, where you are.

You would have enjoyed this: Mary and Bill took me out for coffee a few days after. Trying to keep me busy, you know, my mind diverted from 'morbid' topics. We went to that trendy dessert place over on Strand, you remember, Bill likes their apple pie and ice cream. Anyway, when it was his turn to order, he said to the waitress, 'I'll have your apple pie *à la morte,* please.' Mary gasped, you should have heard her, and suddenly Bill realized what he'd said. He flushed red as a Hammer film and looked at me apologetically. But the waitress thought it was hilarious and kept repeating it as new customers came in. There were jokes about the pie turning green, crawling with worms. We could still hear her shrieking when we left.

In a quiet moment, I can place it, where the sound began. A mere mote, a speck, a period typed and left to float on a blank sheet of paper. The beginning of the end. The siren that swallowed you whole. Such a small thing, at first. An insect whine that learned to bellow on the way, reading the street signs, the house numbers. A black note that opened like space.

Strange, that it stopped here. That ambulance at our door. *Here,* where two (relatively) young people were living in (relative) happiness. Somebody screwed up. Was it you?

How many times did I say, under my breath, because honestly, I didn't mean it, *you fool, you shithead, you stupid prick.*

When I was a child, attending mass, the part I liked best was pounding my chest with my fist and chanting *mea culpa, mea culpa, mea maxima culpa.*

But it wasn't my fault. I wasn't the inventor of this farce, this thriller, just a character like you. The heroine cowering in the corner, her hand clapped like a stranger's hand against her mouth. Face it, you were written out, discarded, a paper man torn in two, a jagged line down the centre. Not a drop spilled.

*A stroke,* they said. A stroke of what? Lightning? A caress, fingers placed lovingly on a vein and squeezing tight, forming a little bonbon of clotted blood? Your speech, how suddenly it skidded out of control, words crashing into one another, unspelling themselves in the air before your startled eyes.

They say when someone is dying, it's like being born. The dying need to be cradled, rocked; they want help, warm hands guiding them out, as they were once welcomed in. You didn't stick around for that, though, did you? It was like you were late for work. Like you couldn't wait to be a skeleton dancing.

When they took you away, I cleaned the fridge. Turned the dial to defrost, and went after the iceberg in the freezer with a screwdriver. I put everything on the counter. Wiped gluey bottles with a dishcloth, discovered a jar of spaghetti sauce that had grown a fur muff of mould, tossed out a stiff heel of French bread. It was in the crisper, what I was after, whatever was rotting in there, filling the house with that smell.

I remember watching out the window a corpulent and strangely clumsy sparrow struggling to settle on a branch, as if you had squeezed yourself into that cozy feathered body – it was bursting with you.

'I know what you're going through.' *Yes.* 'At least he didn't suffer.' *No.* 'You have that to be thankful for.' *Yes.* 'It's all over now.' *No ... yes.* 'Before long, you'll be able to pick up the pieces, start again.' *Yes, the pieces, all over.* Like mercury falling.

You were a swimmer, you had a swimmer's body. You moved through the water like oil, smooth and fast. You shaved your legs, your arms, for the second or two advantage it would give you.

I found this fragment in your desk, I didn't know you collected such things. Rules for where one may play a zither: upon a stone, in the shade of a forest, in a high-ceilinged room, in the moonlight.

You were blue, what do you want me to say?

Your possessions are a weight I have been lifting, slowly. A memento bestowed upon a friend of yours here, a furtive midnight drop at a Goodwill Box there. On someone's wrist, I have seen you walking away, in someone's arms, clinging to their back. You are dispersed beyond regathering. Everyone tries to help in this, descending like a flock of birds picking apart a nest, reapportioning the bits that were yours.

You would have preferred a comic death, I suppose, would have settled for an unusual one: an icicle through the head, a fatal piss in an exploding toilet. Something to distinguish you, afterlife as an anecdote. Some people have all the luck.

As it is, no one wants to speak of you. Your name leaves a bad taste in their mouths. You have become awkward, an unpalatable subject. Maybe they're superstitious, afraid that recalling you will bring you back. Maybe they don't believe in death. The other day, I found a hair on your side of the couch, one of those rare white ones, silver in my palm crossing all the lines – life mind heart.

On the morning you were buried, some man, business-as-usual, called and asked if I wanted to have the funeral videotaped. They were running a special on funerals that week. No kidding.

Produced by, directed by, starring.

So, what's a person supposed to do at a graveside, anyway? There should be concessions, games, planned activities. Like prayer? Something to stop the feet from twitching and shuffling. Life is as strong as death, did you know that? It muscled me, not out of the way, but into it. A person can meditate only so long by a grave, sending their rearing thoughts like trowels into the unresponsive earth. I felt this terrific pull, this force, and the living eyes at my back, and voices saying, *Honey, there's plenty of time for that, come away now, come home, we'll have a few drinks, order some food.*

I stepped into it and it swept me away, into the future, blood pumping, cells working like slaves to keep me going. Scarcely five minutes out of the gate, get this, and someone had me laughing, it came pouring out of my mouth, a magician's trick, like a long and coloured scarf of vomit.

# Oral History

KISSES can be noisy as waterfalls. Light as hosts. Some are bold as flies and carry you away bit by bit. Others, grown cold, gather into drifts in personal history. In the case where few are given or received, a kiss might crystallize and shine in dark memory like a lonely star. Wolves kiss, and some humans kiss like wolves, hungrily. Of course, there will always be those who think about other things while they're kissing – what to make for supper, what to buy for cousin Mimi's birthday – which really isn't nice, or fair. Water kisses the shoreline, sunlight kisses the skin, and it is possible to be kissed by a bullet or a blade. *But,* if it's true satisfaction you're after, a lingering electrifying kiss, then find an honest to goodness mortal and pucker up. A real pair of lips, yes, and not the chill insubstantial ones of some phantom, some shade cajoled out of the woodwork for a late afternoon smooch.

Take Charley Hay, an island boy who worked in the men's department of Nighswander's. Now he was familiar with the fictional dalliance (the yielding lips of pillows, the chaste kiss of glass or stone), and he knew this couldn't compare with the pleasures to be had with Mrs. Huey Putt in the lilac bushes behind the Shaftsbury Hall, her mouth a wide wedge of hot strawberry pie.

Mind you, Charley came to it honestly, hailing as he did from a family of kissers. When his mother and father married, two old established families joined in one large embrace. Affection was a family trait, a language in which kissing served as punctuation as well as conjunction. Nothing began or ended correctly without a kiss. The embarrassed, self-conscious kiss, badly aimed and hastily delivered, was to them as unfortunate as a grammatical slip. Charley's Aunt Beatty once broke off a relationship with an otherwise blameless man on the grounds that *he kissed like a pig.*

An endearing atmosphere was something Charley took for granted as a child. Kisses rained down gently. They healed cuts and staunched tears. He snatched them quickly, like cookies swiped off a plate, before running out to play. And he always went to bed at night with one simmering on his lips. Kisses were what the cat gave with a flick of her rough tongue. What aunts and uncles gave with presents, and whether gin-laced smackers or kisses that sat quietly as scars he scarcely noticed.

But a time came when he had to. A time when he began to hear everywhere, in the flow of wind and water, female voices. A bewitching siren call that filled his ears with a musical nectar, accompaniment to the soft buzz of hormones swarming in his blood.

His mother, eyeing him closely one day, observed, *You're girl crazy.* It was true. He put away his pea shooter, hung up his slingshot, and marched into town, lips ambitiously puckered.

In school Charley experimented widely, harvesting a bounty of first kisses. He necked, pecked, bussed and osculated. He even met his French teacher after class and did it *en français.* He became in short order something of a connoisseur, a collector. While his friends pursued the exotic in stamps or coins, he was busy garnering the unpredictable in that most personal of seals. A kiss is a telling thing, after all, singular as a signature, an accurate register of hidden or disguised feeling. He'd known passion from shy thin lips, emotional thrift from lips full as a purse. A starched and stately woman might deliver a slovenly slipshod kiss, and one pious as a nun could fool you with a kiss of startling and searing intensity.

One thing about Charley, he didn't have to try very hard. Girls loved him and their mothers did too. When Barney Nighswander hired him he knew he'd have a drawing card and was prepared to turn a blind eye to the occasional scuffle among the lamb's-wool sweaters. It baffled him, nonetheless. In his upstairs office, idly punching keys on the adding machine, he would try to tabulate Charley's charms: dazzling blue eyes, golden hair, cherubic face, true all that, but the boy was too obliging, too genial, with a wimp's lapdog look. More a debit that a credit to the gender was Barney's final tally. And yet, given only five minutes in Charley's dark corner of the store, women laden with boxer shorts and ties for their husbands would sweep up to the sales desk, faces glowing as though they had just stepped out of a garden with arms full of fresh-cut flowers. Barney considered himself to be quite the wit, and more than adequately stocked in the looks department, but who had ever approached him with hungry pouting lips? No one. Which made him peck harder at the machine, his mouth pinched tighter than a string bag, *tighter*, Bruce the stockboy, who was a nature-lover, liked to say, *than a canary's arse.*

What moved women in a tide toward Charley? Even those contentedly moored to boyfriends or husbands? Perhaps it was some tantalizing scent or intoxicant of his, some irresistible genetic brew. Or the quarter-moon dimples in his cheeks, and the cleft in his chin, those mesmerizing hooks and curves that formed a devil's triangle around his alluring lips. Whatever the reason, women came away from him untarnished by guilt. A kiss, sweet and simple, wasn't really an infidelity – a little taste possibly, a delicious appetizer. The entanglements of a full-blown affair, a situation is which kissing was quickly debased like a handful of cash strewn on the backseat of a car, he deftly avoided. For Charley, smooching was never a mercenary act, never a warmup to more strenuous exercise. Hips and breasts were all very well, but let someone else wrestle with them was his feeling. His eyes seldom strayed below a woman's chin, and this too may have added to his appeal. His arms were a haven, a retreat from physical measurement and appraisal. You could be stacked like a layer cake or thin as a wafer and still merit a sumptuous soul-stirring kiss from Charley Hay.

Also, he was prudent. His amorous encounters were common knowledge – he was something of a star in the communal daydream – yet this only found covert expression. It ran in murmurs and asides, a thrilling secretive undertone, which, if it broke the surface, would be muffled and deflected by people whispering behind a screen of hands. Charley played his part by carefully tending his reputation. Indiscreet and arrantly stolen kisses were out. Definitely no kissing and telling. Above all, he understood the potency of a kiss. To some, a kiss might not mean very much, might be considered a trifling gesture, antique and laughable, but Charley had more respect for the art than that. He realized that a kiss had power, that it could pack a punch. Just a wee one, sprightly and puckish, quick as a lick, could cause a lot of mischief. It didn't take much to let the furies in – one overly passionate expression of goodwill at New Year's, one incendiary little *smuck*, might turn a dance hall into a boiling mass of arms and fists, a stream of drunks seething like lava into the cold street. Which is why Charley kissed responsibly and with just enough academic interest in the subject to keep him out of trouble.

BUT TROUBLE, too, has a pair of kissable lips and no qualms about promiscuity. It can take you in its dirty, calloused hands, bend you backwards like rubber, pass you around like a shared smoke. Look for it, ask for it, try to *avoid* it, and it'll introduce you with an entrepreneurial wink to the most unlikely customers.

There was this woman who sometimes came into the store. She broke rules as easily as cracking knuckles, was lean as a lizard, and had even leaner ideas about feminine dress and deportment: she slouched, she swore, she smelled *unusual*, the women in Lingerie delicately noted. She could spit clear across the room through the gap in her front teeth and drown a roach that was trying to squeeze under the baseboard on the other side. Then she'd wipe her mouth on her sleeve, which would be a male one, checkered or striped, since she dressed like a man and wore on her face, as if accessorized, a masculine degree of scorn.

The domestic harness – what most women bought with their fund of kisses – was not for her. Hard to imagine even, life carried on behind a broom or a purse. What she liked best was plunging her hands into her pockets and making music with a well of uncounted change as she swaggered down the street. Who was she? Nobody, some punk from out of town, some delinquent on the loose, language hard as muscle, clothes burr-puckered and stained like maps. She wrestled with dogs. No one would have dreamed of romancing her, dreamed of sharing kisses that surely would be like sharing a mouthful of fireflies, like sucking on a light socket. Except Charley.

Something about her mouth nagged him: unkissed, it was a puzzle asking to be solved. He'd made a study of her mouth, and truly, cursing or bullying, it had an enticing mobility. He let it work on his imagination, let it appear before him, provocative, quick to taunt, wearing nothing but a slight smirk. Those lips! In the hothouse of his fantasy they blossomed into curved pink cushions of flesh, pert and busy as an *amoretto*, whispering, snickering, promising the impossible: kisses like ambrosial confections detonating sweetly on his lips, or deeply expressive kisses, tactile works of art, ravishing epics. The range he envisioned was encyclopaedic, with kisses sharp as hooks, wandering kisses that travelled across his face with a tickling swiftness, decorative kisses tiered with feeling, and snail-slow serious kisses that made a career of consonance, stitching (xxxxxxxxxxx) and healing the heart's gashes.

Charley couldn't help but see his lips on hers dancing a labial *pas de deux*.

Violet Winch, over in Notions, could almost see it herself. She was minding her own business, admittedly a tentacled and probing thing, when she caught sight of Charley in the dressing room mirror, stretching and flexing his mouth, then attacking the air with a sensual embouchure. He might have been in training for some kind of oral marathon. Violet was reminded of her own quota of affection – a featherlight jab on the jaw every Saturday night before Al left for the Legion – and of her imaginary lover, a mere wisp of a man, but what a kisser! She'd spent more than a few potent moments beneath the counter consorting with the unseen. What harm was there in that? *Plenty*, the other women in the store might have answered, as they watched a valued public resource being diverted into private and invisible hands. Judas himself with his two-faced kisses couldn't have caused more heartache. Here was a betrayal that upset the emotional ecology of the store and drove something ugly and unclothed out of the depths, an unleashed hostility that stalked the aisles, nipping and pinching, crackling like static, stirring up swirling eddies of anger. Mannequins toppled; dressmaker's pins sank into fat calves like quills; rumour circulated like bad blood; *words* were exchanged.

Barney Nighswander, hit by a tidal wave of customer complaint, fled upstairs to his office where he got his hands on a dimpled bottle that gave him round wet kisses, loyal and long as a dog's throat.

Charley, oblivious to all this, was planning his strategy. To him, the question was no longer hypothetical, but a mere matter of logistics. Should he attempt a subtle advance or a blitz? An ornate kiss dressed in baroque preface, or a bald and brazen one that struck like a snake? He was a messenger with miraculous news to be delivered in a conversation as close as lips would allow. Yes, he would capsize her with a kiss, if only he could get near her.

You might suppose she'd be easy to get hold of, just grab her by the shirt tail, gather up her bantam weight and sink a good one, a direct hit. Impossible: she was slick as a fish; she evaded charm like an insect insulted by light. Drifting into the store, she stopped by Charley's counter to finger the sweaters, the pants, while he erupted into a nervous salesman's patter, concentrating the full force of his attention upon her, his face working like an electric sign advertising inducement. Imagine flirtation so suggestive, so hot, it hurt to watch. Did she notice? Not a bit. He stole looks while she stole merchandise. She brazenly stuffed her coat full then wandered over to some other department, as he gazed after her longingly.

Or tried to. Really, it was becoming hard to see her any more for the potential and inaccessible kiss. The teasing elusive thing had grown to such a size that it loomed, an independent being with pedigree and divine connections. It radiated power and meaning like a sun-sized ciborium. Was central in his narrative as a spell-binding kiss in a fairy tale.

*Do you work here, or what?* were her first words to him. Next it was, *Hey, wake up, will you!*

She was dangling a pair of worksocks in front of his eyes. *How much?*

*A dollar,* Charley fired back, instantly cocking a beckoning eyebrow. What was she doing here, buying something? Maybe it was her feet, not her lips that wanted addressing.

*I'll give you fifty cents.* She flipped a silver coin at him, shoved the socks in her pocket, and sauntered off down the aisle, v's of mud flipping off the bottom of her rubber boots.

*Wait,* it was almost a shout. Charley was getting annoyed, this just didn't happen to him. *You owe me.*

She continued toward the door in no particular hurry. Once there though, she turned to appraise him, a red-faced boy making a pass at indifference, his mouth drawn into a long blank line. She saw this and must have known the answer, what needed to be written there, the finishing touch, since she stepped with such agility out of character, easily as a dress unbuttoned falls to the floor, and blew him a kiss. *She blew him a kiss,* raised her hand, the tips of her fingers to her mouth and launched an airy vessel, a delicate floating seed that followed a whimsical tumbling path to him. Any irony or cruelty her gesture may have contained dissolved in the space travelled between them, so that when the tiny winged kiss reached Charley, bedding down on his lips with a softness of ash, it was almost too fragile to be borne.

She winked once, and was gone.

# Casting Off

WHILE SWALLOWS SWOOP over the house like black jets and starlings kill time in the garden, Valentine knits. On his lap, growing like a beard, is a sweater for his nephew Felice, who lives in Spain and smells of orange blossoms. A quickly melting ball of angel-white wool jitterbugs at his feet. Valentine is a talented knitter, and fast.

That time on the island, the long winter when forty babies had been born one after the other like chickadees tumbling out of the cedars, his hands had moved like wings click-clicking deep into the night, while a great pile of booties and bonnets rose in a quarter moon around his feet. A curious thing, too, how close those children were to one another. The silvery-thin spider's thread that linked them at birth held when they were taken home to farms, fishing camps and reserves. They watched out for one another in their unwinding dreams. At school they regrouped, swelling each grade like the belly of an overstuffed snake. Valentine remembers. He used to see them in town, a knot of ten or twelve running, always running, seeming to draw life out of the grass like a swarm of locusts making a clean sweep. In high school they formed whole hockey and baseball teams that ranged the north undefeated, bewildering the competition with their unfailing instinctive code. They brought home trophies and gold cups filled with beer that sloshed over the sides when passed from hand to hand to hand.

What unpicked the weave? A rumour of war that drifted in with the mist across the channel. Some stayed behind, but most went overseas to fight. A thick fog hugged the house while Valentine knitted rough woollen khaki socks, soon to be shredded in a heaving dissolving landscape. It was death that singled them out, that and grief which joined their private confederacy and led them, one by one, into shadows deeper than the lake.

Valentine shakes his head. He's knitted one sleeve longer than the other. Unravelling, ranging through his past, he thinks of the woman who taught him this skill. His grandmother, Claire Purvis. She had large strong hands that gathered in warmth like a bear, and could, she bragged, knit ten man-sized mitts in a day and put the thumbs in after supper. She was originally a Devlin, last of the seven Devlin girls and the only one born on the island. Her parents and sisters had travelled up from London to home-stead, coming over the lake on the steamer *Manitou.* Described as a spunky little boat, the *Manitou* entertained one bad habit – fire. During a moment of extreme tension or excitement on board she would burst into flames. It was commonly believed that she was built of wood grown in hell. She'd gone down once already as the *Aurora,* taking twenty-odd souls with her, then had been raised and renamed. But the experience hadn't altered her character much. On the day the Devlins crossed the lake, a party of Jesuits were also on board, which made everyone nervous and not the least bit surprised when tongues of fire started licking sleeves and nesting in hair. By the time the *Manitou* blazed into port, passengers were hurling themselves overboard. The Devlin girls burned their hands sliding down a fiery rope over the bow. On the other side of the bay, Sampson Abotossaway painted the whole event in miniature, the steamer flaming like a jewel, the Devlins a string of pearls dropping into the water. Their palms were severely scarred, their life and mind and heart lines forever melded and obscured, turned into an abstract art useful as tangled fishline. Sensing trouble ahead, the Devlin parents made room for another child, one with faultless, capable, and encom-passing hands to look after them all. And that was Claire.

Valentine doesn't ever recall seeing his grandmother's hands empty or at rest, or masked in white gloves like the hands of her sisters. For a lifetime her hands worked, clenching a hammer or a cow's teat, carrying endless buckets of water or bowls of soup, stroking a hot feverish head, holding back a brimming madness. She had accumulated power in those hands. Valentine felt it like a presence, heard it purr and crackle beside him as he lay in bed brightly dotted with measles or swollen toad-faced with mumps.

Her hands moving continuously, pleaching bay and leaf-coloured wool into a blanket that spread out in waves around her, and her yarning voice, also continuous, reminded him of water lapping against the dock and had the same hypnotic effect. He slipped like an elver in and out of sleep and what she told him those dark and tree-wild rainy afternoons seemed to flow easily, seamlessly into his dreams.

Valentine closed his eyes and saw a man thundering down the road, burly and tough as a voyageur, lightning in his eyes and on his tongue. It was Father Papineau roaring to his black matched team of Tony-on-Time horses. Father Papineau was a raving wind that lashed the parish – his masses turbulent, his sermons full of exploding exhortation. He hadn't learned the whispering of priests, the soft and secretly delivered absolution. The walls of the confessional shook when he was in it. With anger, or laughter, depending on the nature of the sins being confessed. One time he ploughed his arms through the confessional screen and choked a man. For penance, he explained afterward, with a smile like a whip.

Father Papineau was tucked like a black boiling cloud between Claire's storm stories and her freak stories. He followed the sinking of the *Asia*, seventy people drowned and whitecaps standing tall as men on the lake, and preceded Golly McClay's scramble-faced Herefords, born on Hallowe'en night with nostrils beneath their jaws, and the story of the Devlin cousin in the navy whose eyes popped out of his head one day and lay like small soft-boiled bird's eggs on his cheeks.

On the edge of all this ranged Taibeness, a medicine man with the Obidjewong, a band that lived near the Devlin farm. He could communicate with stones, she said, and send his thoughts darting like dragonflies across the water. He was a healer; he could take any dying creature in his hands and give it life. His appearance and abilities were well matched. He was unusually tall, with a river of reddish hair flowing like lava down his back, and a growth about three inches long on the top of his head that resembled a horn. *Honestly,* said Claire. Valentine didn't doubt

it. Everyone feared Taibeness, and with reason. His curses falling like an axe could split you in two. Fortunately he liked Claire.
He got used to her presence and pestering questions, and even
admired the canny wolf's eyes set in such a plain and honest
child's face. He was the one who taught her their language. She
picked it up quickly, deftly lacing the words he gave her into sentences sturdy as baskets, deep in their understanding, and in
these the Obidjewong placed their trust. She was allowed
glimpses into their world not usually given to whites. Through
cracks opened for her in the sky and in the earth she saw powerful spirits. She was shown in rivers shimmering golden-eyed fish
that had once been human. Valentine listened, breathless, his
doggy boy's hair bristling, as she told him about the great snake
god, and about the dead who walk in the woods at night, faceless
and nameless. With a soul-catcher carved out of bone, Taibeness drew maps on the ground, illustrating a network of sacred
trails that ran like veins over the island. Settlers were severing
them, he said, with their houses and roads. He would look at her,
confused as a bleeding man, and ask, what kind of people are
they that beat snakes to death with clubs? Then he'd say, the
world is falling apart and my hands are no longer strong enough
to hold it together.

*Can that happen,* Valentine wanted to know, *can the world fall
apart?*

*Oh yes,* his grandmother would answer, still knitting, placid as
a cat on a hearth. *Yes, indeed. Like the time* ... and she'd go on to
tell Valentine about her first husband Bedeau McGovern who
broke everything in sight, including the frail hearts of Claire's
sisters. He wasn't really a bad boy, she'd claim, just wild. He
liked to put his hands on a woman and stir her up like a pool. He
liked to see long hair undone, spilling over shoulders, down
backs. Something he wanted to find in the very centre of things.
Made him act funny, cruel sometimes. He killed meticulously,
taking animals apart with surgical skill, fingers so sensitive he
could read and dispel the finest lines in creation. He'd undo anything – would unweave sparrows' nests, bugger jigsaws, spin

mother's good china plates through the air. Brand new machinery, purchased with egg money saved for years, he disassembled in seconds. He did the same to clocks, gutting them, then holding a disarray of tiny wheels in his palm like a clutch of deer's teeth. He turned time around. After Claire married Bedeau, who could even remember what day it was? Though all the McGovern boys were like that. *Damn fools,* her father said, recalling at the wedding how they harrowed his garden with their bootheels, stubbing out the bright fiery heads of flowers. The McGoverns used to take their mother with them when they went out hunting and make her run through the bush to scare out the animals. They'd shoot at anything, no matter how small.

Of all the deaths imaginable for Bedeau, and people did imagine them – saw him being torn apart by wolves, legs and arms carried off in every direction, his blood spelling a final, frantic and unintelligible message on the ice, or they imagined his heart going off like a bomb and the roiling chaos inside splattering out and eating into everything like acid – of all the deaths that were dreamed, his real one seemed the least likely. A black horse, bought from the gypsies camped on Boozeneck Road, kicked him. But lightly, barely touching Bedeau on the temple with its hoof. It took his life away from him so easily, sweetly, as one dark prince might steal a kiss from another. Claire was stunned, as though she herself had been knocked down. She carried him into the house, for once calm in her arms. They washed and dressed him on the kitchen table, then laid him in the parlour, natty in a pin-stripe suit, riotous hair slicked back. A tiny violet bruise-blossom on the side of his head. His warmth scarcely gone. Claire's sisters whimpered around him, and he seemed to tease them, his lips poised on the verge of telling a secret. Though he told them nothing, Claire said, and stayed out of their dreams, and looked more pleased with himself than a dead man should.

After Bedeau there was another – Morgan Purvis. He brought a trickle of Welsh blood into the family, seven fiddle tunes (including 'Barney Google', the sisters' favourite), two pet beavers, Jim and Queenie, and a moose named Viola. This husband was tame and soft as flannel, with a mild unvarying temper, though was not without his own magic. He knew a verse in the Bible that if spoken backwards stopped a cut from bleeding. He had pockets full of peppermints and a heart, everyone said, as big as the moon. He was the kind of grandfather you could nuzzle into on a hurtful day and be healed. And although it's true that Claire loved her first one, the wild boy, best, she knew that Morgan, working in the half-light, industrious as a squirrel, had unearthed the future for her to compose.

Outside Valentine's place the trees are alive with jays and the lawn is studded with blue windfall plums. A gust of children skitters by, mouths stopped momentarily with candy. The neighbours are thinking of leaves to rake and of the coming cold, and as they sit down to lunch their thoughts meet and run together like watercolours.

Valentine finishes his knitting, casting off the last of the stitches, then holds up his nephew's sweater to admire. *Perfect*, he has to admit. As he gets up to search for brown paper and string, a cloud shifts in the sky and suddenly, before him, light dances a dazzling flamenco across the floor.

# Her Toes

TEN! *What* bounty! Paris couldn't count that far, but he knew numbers when he saw them. Dearth was ear lobes, chewy delicacies when you could get them; scarcity was nipples, twin pink stars hung too high, halfway to heaven and spied only at night when Momma was undressing for bed. But toes, *her toes*, came in tumbling footfalls, in rooting litters, piggies popping out of socks, close and many, something a boy could actually reach out and touch. And sink his teeth into. If he had any.

*Yow!* The big ones knocked him flat every time. Sudden as eel faces poking out the dark holes at the end of her fuzzy pink slippers. Paris would make a grab for one, and back in it would scoot. Missed again! What a gas! That's if Momma was in a good mood, playful as she sometimes was. Catch her in a nasty one and you might get a kick in the face. Momma was like the weather and Paris took what he got. It all came from her, succouring warmth and chilly blasts, she was everything. *Hell, I'm just a stupid baby,* he would think, wondering if he was old enough to have that thought, old enough to hurt himself on words.

Frustration? He couldn't even walk, his toes were little rudders guiding him through the channels of the house, rubbery nubs that helped him scooch across the floor. Of course this made him easy pickings for the Lerch women, his hulking aunts who swooped down and scooped him up before he could squirm to safety behind the couch. They held him nose-length from their wet blubbering lips making kissy-face, and *my God* they were ugly! He stared, feeling faint, at large greasy pores and teeth that loomed like tombstones. Paris feared that one day, when Momma wasn't looking, they'd gobble him up. 'Gonna eat your tummy,' they'd chortle, and his face would crumple and give way like paper on fire.

'Gracious, Marilyn,' they complained, 'you're spoiling this child rotten. He's turning into a real wimp.'

'He's making strange.' Momma didn't sound overly concerned.

'But we're not *strangers*. We're *blood*. You know, it's a mercy Gord isn't here to see what's becoming of his son.'

This was the usual load being dumped and Momma didn't bother to answer. Instead, she tapped a cigarette out of her pack of Kools and picked her lighter up off the floor with her toes. A habit, *two* habits, she knew her sisters-in-law deplored.

Her toes were long and misshapen, though dextrous, the stouter kin of her fingers. She opened cupboards with them, turned knobs on the stove. Did the dusting. Picked up blocks and threw them. Momma just naturally reached for things with her feet, ruffled Jet's fur, tickled Paris under the arm. Scratched herself. Her toe-nails were painted fire-engine red and filed to an edge. And didn't Paris know it, scoring his tongue on them as he might on a razor-sharp blade of grass.

He liked to *bam* his chubby hand down on her left and slightly bigger foot where the toes had grown in a tossed heap clambering piggyback on top of one another. In his view, he was helping her straighten them out, making them match the more regularly spaced toes on the other foot. But *bam* every time he flattened them, they'd spring right back into their oddly squashed assembly. 'Stop that!' Momma would get exasperated. 'Can't you leave my feet alone?' No, he couldn't. He *adored* them. They were his icons. His objects of worship, and the only way he could pray to them was to cling and nuzzle and suck. And when they strode away from him, in motion so sleek and strong, but in anger slapping the floor so hard, he cried and cried in panic and couldn't stop.

The Lerch feet were something else. Ballooning appendages stuffed bulging into shoes too tight – toes with cleavage! He was always anxious that their feet were going to explode and gag him with rags of flying flesh. He'd been made to ride-a-cock-horse on one of those feet, straddling ankles like hips, and he'd nearly died of fright. 'Wheeeee!' the Lerches screeched, mistaking his terror-stricken face for one stung with pleasure.

They clattered through the house in their black shoes, crunching up broken glass on the floor.

'Marilyn! The baby could hurt himself on this! Where's the broom? You do *have* a broom, don't you?'

'Yeah, sure, I don't ride mine.'

The Lerches were like that. Not too subtle. When Paris was born, Granny Lerch, herself the mother of triplets, said to Momma, 'Just the *one*, I suppose?' But Momma gave as good as she got. She bared a milky breast as if to feed him (another revolting habit), and pinged Granny on the chin with a warm thin squirt.

Where was Gord when his son was born, that's what Momma wanted to know. 'What do you expect,' they said. 'It's hunting season.'

Paris himself was a hunter. That one time anyway when the house filled up with a forest of legs and he meandered among them on the trail of something sweet. So many voices high above reminded him of birds singing in the treetops, repeating the same few notes, *Sorry, sorry, we're so sorry.* Someone dropped a half-eaten sandwich and he crammed it in his mouth before Jet could get to it. Under the coffee table he discovered a wad of hard pink gum, which he pried loose, and on top of the table a glass of watery rye. Both excellent. He ate a pickle dressed in dog hair, two buttons, and most of a shoelace that got yanked back out by Aunt Mona Lerch. Paris was able to avoid his aunts for the most part, veering away from their hairy legs that were packed like pressed bushes into stockings and planted like monuments throughout the room. If only he'd kept his mouth shut when the green man appeared at the window.

As usual, this took Paris by surprise. 'Da da,' he said, and it was like a knife plunged into the Lerches' hearts.

'Oh!' gasped Fern Lerch. 'He *knows*. Poor little pumpkin.'

'Instinct,' claimed Reola Lerch. 'You can't fool babies or animals. They *just know*. Look at Jet. Have you ever seen anything more pathetic?'

Gord's mangy old hound did indeed look poorly. He had

lapped up a bowl of Lerch chip dip that was catfighting in his stomach.

'Nonsense,' Momma said, stepping out of her shoes and examining a blister on her heel. 'He always says that. Doesn't mean a thing. It's baby talk.'

'Well, I suppose,' said Mona Lerch, 'that *under* the circumstances, you might find it a comfort to think so.'

THE CIRCUMSTANCES were weighing most heavily on Jet, as he was under the misapprehension that he was dead. Not from the chip dip. He had already passed on when he'd gobbled that up, figuring he could hazard it.

Even a dog can count to two – two wags of the old tail, two scratches behind the ear, two barks 1) *woof* 2) *woof* – and he had definitely counted *two* shots. One that levelled Gord, a gusher of blood oozing from his chest, and the other that killed him. He'd hit the dirt, in any case. Hunting accident? Jet wasn't so sure. How anyone could mistake Gord for a deer was beyond him. (A bear, maybe.) Of course everything was beyond him now. And the part that really bugged him about dying was how little things had changed. You'd think, in afterlife, that a limitless supply of food would drift down like manna into a golden dog dish. Hah! Think again. He got the *same* meagre scoop of soybean-extended goop plopped into the *same* unwashed bowl that the very *same* toothless drooling baby stuck his hands into and licked when his mother (the *same*) wasn't watching (which was most of the time). Then the door would burst open and a herd of those enormous women who had tormented him for years would thunder through the house for no other reason, it seemed, than to tromp on his tail. Jet had not expected injustice to have a supernatural dimension, to skew his chances at some kind of otherworldly betterment. Evidently it was a dog's life *and* a dog's death.

PARIS HAD no idea what was going on, but he sure liked it. Momma had emerged from behind a cloud of blue smoke, grinning, sunny side up. 'Sweetie,' she said, 'look.' And she wedged pennies between her toes and wiggled them. She astonished him by painting faces on them with eyebrow pencil and lipstick, giving them personalities and histories, family troubles told in tiny voices that lisped and squeaked. Grief had worked wonders on her. Used to be, you could never tell with Momma. Paris had seen things written on her lovely face that stopped him dead. Baleful wounding words reflected in a script of scowl and frown. You didn't have to know how to read to get the message: *Shut up, you make me sick. Get lost, I don't want you. You've ruined my life. I wish you'd never been born. You were a mistake. You're bad bad bad.*

But there'd been a carefree unravelling of the scowl, the frown. Her look had been revised to one of collusion, of private fun, that made him pump his arms in wild excitement. 'Hey rug rat, watch this!' She plunged her foot into the peanut bowl and nuts spun in the air as she tried to catch them in her mouth. Paris laughed and laughed. He wanted to do it too. He made a grab for a stray peanut, got it in his mouth, and choked on it. Momma had to hold him up by the heels and whap him on the back until – *pop!* – out it flew and bounced off Jet's nose. This made *her* laugh and that was the best of all. She whirled him round and round by the feet, until his delighted shrieks turned into screams and tears ran all over his bald head like ants and the room became a spinning drain that sucked him down into darkness.

THE LERCHES were plotters and schemers. Benign ones if they were cooking up a surprise party or a bridal shower, but not always so. At times they felt it necessary, for moral reasons, to take on the exacting work of a less pleasant design. In a huddle, in cozening secrecy, they discussed the fate of their nephew, the unsuitability of his mother, *what* was to be done.

PARIS WAS oblivious to intention, harmless or otherwise, even nature's. Momma set him loose in the back garden and he found the patterns changed somehow – things looked different. He tasted some spider webs that were like cotton candy and sampled a dead bee. He spent a considerable amount of his time and patience improving a bush, attempting to reattach its fallen pinky-shaped leaves. It appeared the bush was broken and he hoped he hadn't done it. A ribbon of wind brought the green man (*boo!*), who had a snack for Paris slung over his mossy shoulder. Carrots, the way Paris loved them, with clumps of earth still clinging to the rootlets. The green man ate the tops. Paris sat by his grass-stained feet and studied the lichen on his legs, while the green man stroked Paris's head and hummed in his ear. A sad song, Paris thought, as it was getting cold and the green man had no clothes.

Momma was watching Paris through the window. He was sitting still as a statue, gazing beatifically into space. He's seeing angels, she thought, or ghosts. Babies have those kinds of visionary powers, she believed, and they're smarter than you think. She was positive he wasn't seeing Gord or he'd be bawling his head off. *Jesus!* When Paris was all of three days old, Gord bought him a toy gun. Kid couldn't even focus his eyes yet, and here was this idiot hovering above the crib, gun shoved into the blue plush head of a teddy bear, saying, 'See, son, like this ... BAM BAM!' When he was old enough to grab things, Momma had to take it away from him, he kept bonking himself on the head with it and got a nasty welt.

'Cripes, if he's dumb enough to do that,' Gord had said, 'he deserves it. Teach him a lesson. School of hard knocks, that's how I was brung up.'

Ah, yes, the Lerch educational system. It had produced some real gems. Lerch logic? It was bent like a boomerang and Momma was sick of being hit with it. 'Let the baby cry,' Gord's sisters were adamant. 'It's good for his lungs.'

'Uh-huh,' she'd say, gathering him up and holding him close. At least there'd be no more crying now, she thought.

Momma felt a shiver, like a cold finger, running up her spine and she wheeled around. It was Jet, staring daggers at her. Over the days he'd been splicing odd bits of evidence together, adding one plus one, and it hadn't been easy. But he had it all worked out, he had dredged up the answer. *Thump, thump, thump, thump* went his tail on the floor like a judge's gavel. That flash of a familiar green garment he saw in the bush, and later, the smell of gunpowder on that woman's hands. *Where were you the afternoon Gord was shot?* his cool probing eyes asked Momma.

Momma smiled at him, and said, 'Dead dog.'

Then she turned back to the window to check on Paris. But he was gone. *Vanished.*

DOCTOR JACK was instructed to look for what the Lerches were convinced he would find. The stigmata of abuse. Bruises concealed beneath clothing, cuts, slashes, cigarette burns on the bottom of feet. They wanted him to witness, deeply etched on the child's skin, the whole painful proof of his martyrdom in *that* house.

'*Not* a soul watching him,' said Fern Lerch.

'Had *mud* streaming out of his mouth,' said Reola Lerch.

'Was about to *eat* poison berries before I knocked them out of his hand, poor dear,' said Mona Lerch.

She'd smacked Paris hard, too. His hand hurt like the devil. Couldn't they tell the berries weren't for him? Yew berries? He *knew* better than that, Momma had already warned him about them. No, they were a gift for the green man. He would suck the light out of the sweet fruit lanterns and spit out the seeds. Paris had been so absorbed in picking the berries that he didn't notice the conjoined amorphous Lerch shadow fall over the fence. The green man had tried to warn him, grimacing and waving his pale fingers in fright, but they bundled Paris off and stuffed a mitt in his mouth before he could work up a decent scream.

'Ladies, I don't think I've ever seen a healthier kid,' said Doctor Jack. 'Now, he's got a bit of an *orange* tinge. But that's carrots, you know, too many carrots will do that. You tell Marilyn to cut down on them. Otherwise, I'd say she's doing a great job with this boy.'

'But what about the *marks?*'

'Oh, *those.* Well, if you don't mind my saying so, I don't

believe he'll be getting those any more. If you know what I mean? My condolences, by the way.'

'We can't imagine what you're insinuating, Doctor,' said Mona Lerch, snapping her purse shut, 'but a father's *got* to discipline his son.'

KIDNAPPED.

Paris was doing his best to make life miserable for the perpetrators of the crime. To stop his screaming, Reola jounced him around like a pinball in her arms and he deposited a slimy hill of regurgitated carrot on her plank of shoulder. He filled his diaper as fast as they could change it, kicking and cycling his pudgy little legs, while Fern struggled to hold him down. He caught her between the eyes with a sudden spurt of pee and she was so shocked she drove the safety pin into her thumb. She ran squealing from the room and Paris rolled off the wardrobe clutching a jar of Vaseline, huge gobs of which he was then able to massage into the rug.

Paris hoped he'd be able to keep these tactics up until Momma came to fetch him. He didn't plan on staying in this funhouse any longer than he had to. He felt a strange force here, as though something had him by the cheeks. As though his babysoft face were being pulled and tugged out of shape, and he was being remoulded in *their* likeness. Everyone in this place looked the same to him, even Puff Lerch, their fat, irritable cat that took a swat at him when he'd yanked its tail. *No sense of humour.* That's what Momma would say. A family trait. And family was everything to the Lerches, Momma said, though they didn't realize they were sealed in theirs like a tomb. *You'd think family was some kind of weapon the way they use it to bludgeon outsiders.* Momma could really get going sometimes, her feet pacing back and forth, back and forth, her toes clenching and curling when she stopped to drive a point home. And Gord bouncing up and down, sizzling hot 'cause he couldn't put two words together to save his soul.

Where *was* he, anyway? Paris half expected him to leap out of a closet, roaring, making those monster faces that terrified him. That made him cringe and shake. A response that Gord seemed to want. And not want. A response that brought the pain, the punishment. Swift and hard, like being put to sleep under a stone blanket.

Paris decided to scoot under a table. He was attracted by a brown thing on Grampa Lerch's leg. A mole, but to him it passed for a crumb of chocolate and he thought he might try to pick it off and eat it. Apparently they didn't believe in feeding babies here, and he supposed he would have to fend for himself. If nothing else, he had a wicked set of fingernails. Momma usually chewed them down for him, keeping them trim, but she hadn't gotten around to that recently.

MOMMA WAS TARDY. 'I'm late,' she said, finally breezing in, forgetting that she was furious with the Lerches. She threw down a bag of stuff on the floor and kicked off a pair of new purple high-heeled shoes. 'Been out shoplifting,' she announced, grabbing an apple out of the fruit bowl. She took a bite and promptly tossed it over her shoulder. 'Woody,' she said, disgusted, then twirled around a couple of times. *Nice dress*, Paris thought, *made of wind and leaves. And look! Her toes, dancing!*

'Goo, goo,' he said, and immediately regretted it.

'Why, honey,' her voice turned sharp, 'what a cliché. You've been here a couple of hours and already you're talking like them, I can't believe it. And what are you doing tied to the leg of that chair? Wait a minute, who in the hell tied my baby up?'

Momma remembered now – she was furious. 'What are you bunch trying to pull here, anyway? Sneaking around my back yard and *stealing* my kid. I could have you all arrested. *And* shot,' she added. Momma always exaggerates, but the thought seemed to please her, and she started smiling again.

'Good grief, Marilyn, there's no reason to fly off the handle,' said Mona. 'We were simply trying to help you out, give you some time to yourself. Didn't want to bother you, we *know* how you've suffered.'

Momma rolled her eyes and Paris gurgled.

She noticed that Fern was sitting in a corner watching TV and sucking her thumb. Reola was attending to Grampa Lerch, patting his shoulder and cooing in his ear. He had a swath of bandage wound around his leg and was snivelling into his sleeve. *Feed him to the cat*, about summed up Momma's sentiment.

'If you want my advice,' said Mona, 'that boy of yours needs a firm hand. You better show him who's boss, or you'll be sorry.'

'Do tell,' said Momma, lighting up a Kool and crouching down to untie Paris from the bowleg Lerch chair (even their furniture looked like them). Smoke wreathed her face in vaporous thorns. When his hands were freed, Paris reached out to brush them away. She squinted at him and his heart hopped like a frog in his chest.

'That's Gord's old baby harness,' said Mona. 'You can have it if you want.'

'No, thanks.' Momma tucked Paris under her arm, then collected up her shoes and bag of stuff, securing them under the other. 'Say bye bye, Paris.'

'Da da,' Paris said.

Then Momma raised her foot and grasped the doorknob with her toes. Her unnatural, malformed monkey toes, the Lerches thought. Her wondrous, her divine toes, Paris thought. My *useful* toes, Momma thought, opening the door with one expert twist of the knob and sailing right through.

# Quickening

A CREATURE burrowed up through the earth, pushed into the lodge through a loose floorboard in the closet, and walked down the hall into the living room breathing balls of fire that landed like tossed sunwheels on the couch, in the curtains. I was five and carrying my losses to date lightly, easily. Then something got Remy. A grey tabby dispersed like ash. That he had 'wandered off' was the official word. I couldn't believe it. Not Remy. Not from me.

We were away that winter living north of the Island in a small French town, collectively chaperoning my wayward grandfather. He liked women, especially, for some reason, women named Ethel, and had cornered one in this zit of a place where Remy strangely took his leave. My parents resisted cross-examination on the subject, exchanging those knowing looks – to me damningly guilty – when I questioned them. I suspected other cats of being Remy in disguise, that cunning animal, and followed them around the neighbourhood. Marmalade or black as a bat, I missed his warm weight in my hands, his idling motor in my ear at night. I missed his claws, his stripes – he stepped out of them like a cage. Perhaps he disappeared into the language, the French none of us could speak.

My brother was having his own troubles in school because of this. Not fights, but academic disgrace. After a distinguished year in grade one on the Island, his star clearly rising, he was now in rapid descent, clutching a report card that bled red ink as he stumbled shamefaced through the door. His first real taste of failure. Mine of adult duplicity. Two kids sucking on aspirins was how we looked.

My grandfather had a mischievous giggle and like Elizabeth Taylor he believed in marriage. He must have been talked out of it this time though, as there were no nuptials to celebrate, no bride of fifty or sixty grinning down at me with large lipstick-flecked teeth. Celebration in general was muted that winter. In memory, deleted. Christmas is completely gone, though I do remember going to midnight mass at Easter, slipping out into the dark, sleep-deprived and dressed like a piece of candy. It was freezing. The ground was stiff, an alien surface. The wind slapped my new frilly hat into the bushes. Out there, alone, I heard a distant plaintive pinprick of sound. Remy. Crying. I called to him, loudly, voice breaking, over and over, trying to draw him back, desperately playing on the twisted thread of his lost self. Until finally the wind shoved his sweet springing name down my throat and someone grabbed my hand, cold and clawed like a tiny branch, and pulled me into the truck.

A cat can be made to vanish in any number of foul ways: under the wheels of a car, a schoolyard hanging (monkey bars are useful for this), in a tied and weighted sack dropped in a lake, a dog chasing instinct into a dark corner, a human doing research, a drawing and quartering so secret you can't even find the bones and blood. I was five but I wasn't a fool – what the years add to knowledge of cruelty is only detail.

The lodge that stood on the hill with flames growing out of its roof like wild red hair was our home on the Island. We returned in the spring to watch it burn. An entertaining event for some, with stored boxes of fireworks going off and exploding ammunition singing through the air. My parents and I missed the raging part and caught the tail end, a few lazy tongues finishing off the black carcass.

My brother and grandfather, who had come back a week earlier to open up the camp, saw the whole thing, *from A to izzard,* my grandfather said, pretending to be an old man. That morning they'd been driven out of bed, choking on smoke, yet managed to find their boots and throw on coats over their striped PJs before bolting out the door. My grandfather also stopped briefly to gaze at himself in the hallway mirror. This may have been out of habit, or more likely to assess the effect of fiery clouds billowing behind him. A striking figure. *The very devil himself,* he must have thought.

The ice was still in the bay. The ones who live below, the green-haired women with blue bodies and flowing black dresses, would have been gazing up as through a thick distorting window at my brother. Determined to save the lodge, he was hacking at the ice with his Roy Rogers pocket knife, an empty pail beside him. The volunteer fire department from town had taken the wrong road and when they eventually arrived were in a partying mood, wanting more to dally with the fire than quench it.

We lost everything. Even our clustered fingerprints were nibbled off before the furniture and walls were consumed. A detective snooping around would not have found much material evidence of our existence. My mother's documented past, her treasured life in the old country, highland-flinged itself right out of view wearing her Uncle Alec's Black Watch kilt and bearing away an armful of photographs, bedevilling memory. She covered her face with her empty hands, as adults do, and wept. I turned away, taking stock of my blazing tricycle and smouldering bed, my dolls nothing now but a scattered fistful of charred and cracked eyes.

We lost everything, but somehow were no less burdened. Before leaving the Island that winter my father had transferred the insurance from the lodge to the new cottage he was building above the ice house, not being able to afford both. The fire was attracted to the wrong place, so all we got out of it were a few good stories and some crude hunks of metal and glass, my brother's former penny and marble collections melded together into a kind of collector's parody. The situation wasn't completely hopeless, of course; some things you can never lose no matter what. The Aelick boys from the neighbouring farm had rushed into the flames and, with an unerring eye for the peripheral and useless, had rescued a number of items: a waffle iron that produced black inedible objects, the box of tackle containing lures that made even the fish snort derisively, and the two yard-high yellow-eyed ceramic hawks my mother had inherited from the first Ethel and had been trying to get rid of for years.

I had always liked those birds, admiring their crafty

demeanour, and was glad to have one in my arms, warm from the fire, as my brother and I carried them like resident gods down to our new home, the cottage with the insurance. Wonderment is their element, those in the water that is, and they would have watched us coming down to them in a dream, half-bird we must have seemed through the ice. The cottage, fragrant with raw lumber, smelled like the inside of a tree. We claimed our rooms, planting a guardian hawk in each, then ran out the door and up branching paths to the other cottages – Pine Crest, Mayferg, Waubuno, Twin Elms, Americana, But n' Ben, Dewdrop Inn, Sunset – to search for bedding and dishes and whatever it is that a family needs.

Our lives had now shifted closer to the water where I'd get *their* insinuating music in my ears and never get it out.

We had something to see through the picture window in our living room, unlike most people who have them. Not tiny squares of grass and asphalt, but this great expanse, the bay opening into the lake. *Whadaview!* our guests the tourists said, blind to what we saw. What was really out there, shifting and gleaming, wearing scales of light, a mutable skin, a disturbing depth. Daily as prayer we had this in our eyes washing them clean, whetting them to a keen sharpness. We lived beside the water as beside an enormous and unpredictable parent who might buoy you up murmuring in your ear, or pull you under, plugging your nose and mouth with mud, binding you with slime-green weeds. In the evening the lake caught the sun's fire, which made everyone gasp, *whadasight!* while the women swimming less visibly below helped us skip the stones we threw by reaching up with long blue fingers and keeping them alight on the surface.

Our first phone call in the new place came in the middle of the night. We'd been hanging around the kitchen all day, ready to pounce if the thing rang – it was also our first telephone – but were helplessly mired in sleep when it did. My father was the one who struggled up out of bed and answered with a boyish smile that sprang nimbly enough to his lips for three a.m. A minute later it was gone, like the silver flicker of a minnow darting into deep water. We didn't see it again for weeks until the tourists started arriving and it had to be coaxed back onto his face for the sake of business. The call was from my grandfather. He was honeymooning in Cleveland with his new bride, an Ethel Lafleur from Sheguiandah, a woman he'd met at the fire and someone he'd been courting secretly since then.

This Ethel, with her tightly permed calico hair and leathery tough hide, was a slightly bizarre version of the type though to me she came to epitomize Ethelness. She wore thick stockings held up by unreliable elastics, had a chipped front tooth angled like a fang, and a blue-black tongue from chewing endlessly on jawbreakers. My parents were horrified. By her and by her house which was layered with dust and mildew and was as densely packed with curious objects as a museum. I had never before seen hair wreaths and framed fish skin. And she had dolls, old scary ones, that she kept up an active relationship with – her 'babies' that stared like the dead at my brother and me while adult conversation, which usually swished so briskly above our heads, stopped and started like a machine that just wouldn't work. At infrequent but unavoidable Sunday dinners, she served salmon cakes (*sucker,* my father claimed) and mashed potatoes with black lumps entombed in them like flies. My grandfather was the only one who could relax and apparently enjoy these get-togethers, his attraction to his wife solid and not to be fathomed.

*Just wanted to let you know,* he shouted over the phone from Cleveland, this chased by his characteristic chuckle that bubbled into my father's ear like frothing champagne.

Sibling rivalry in my grandfather's family was conducted on a theological battlefield. One brother was a Presbyterian, the other a Methodist. Of his sisters, May attended the United Church, Maude the Anglican, while Minnie met with her friends down at the Kingdom Hall. They had divided up Christianity like so many flavours of ice-cream and fought among themselves about the merits of each. My grandfather, with the sheer delight of annoyance written like a signature into all his motives, was for a long time uncommitted to any faith, until one day he unexpectedly became a Catholic. A trump card that made everyone, even the Jehovah's Witness, howl.

So we were Catholics too, though not the kind I think the Church envisioned when it considered its flock. My father remained skeptical, giving the minimum of devotion, while my mother, who grew up in a place where Catholic meant street gangs and beatings, entered the church like an infiltrator. It suited some aspects of my brother's character, as he enjoyed collecting the medals and holy cards and putting in flawless performances as an altar boy. As for me, it abetted my credulity. I have a talent for belief the way some people have a talent for embezzlement or shoplifting. It gave me licence. If you're going to open the door to sundry saints and angels, then why not the *pah-eens*, those tiny Indian tricksters who lived in the rocks, or the women in the water who spoke a submerged patois that drifted through the windows at night while lichen-scabbed imps, round as owls, curled up in the branches outside?

Priests called on us, though not for the sake of our dodging souls. They came to the camp to relax, to release their eccentricities like dogs that needed a good run in the country. They kept a respectful distance from the unholy water, crossing themselves against it, while at the same time dealing fearlessly with the other fluid elements my parents had on hand. Our hospitality was reciprocated by their own brand of generosity. Almost any spiritual perk could be ours for the asking. If they drank too much, they got reckless and would dispense blessings like pie-eyed fairy godmothers. Trigger-happy, they sanctified the toaster, the shot glasses, the Crest Hardware calendar – once Father Donnelly winged a fly in midair – on and on until our kitchen grew hazy and numinous with grace, more sacred than the Vatican itself.

I had trouble with sin. I just couldn't get the hang of it. Later on, after I'd received First Communion and was old enough to go to confession, I began inventing sins for myself. Diving into transgression as into a fictional dirtpile, smudging my soul in imitation of a typically fallible child. Our teacher depicted the soul as a milk bottle, shaded in spots or completely black, with the spanking clean bottle being the ideal, full to the brim with grace. But we weren't expected to attain it. Who would believe me if I told them I never sinned? So I aimed for liveliness and variety within a venial range, the fine embroidery of small iniquities – untruths and petty thefts and impure thoughts – wanting to give the confessor some entertainment without incurring an overly punishing and time-consuming penance. *Bless me Father for I have sinned,* whispered in the dim confessional to the shadowy figure behind the screen was my cue to improvise, to deliver the goods like a double agent spreading lies about lies.

I saved the truth, the real confessions, for the women in the lake. I knew this about them, that they wept and sang. That they prophesied. What I wanted was help. Perhaps sympathy. Speaking underwater slowly like a record on the wrong speed, I asked them for Remy. I did; they gave him to me in dreams, a cat with fire in its mouth and sparks flying from its tail. He stood on my chest lightly as a sparrow. Though at other times with a suffocating pressure, sodden and unbearably heavy. They were midwives. They pulled him out of the water and placed him in my arms (a stink of death rising). He was their poetry; they delivered him in their devious tongue, translating him into something I couldn't understand. I learned this about them, that they exact tribute. They had dull eyes, not to be read. You might catch a glimpse of them, a trailing limb, the unnatural hue of their skin, a tendril of hair like floating crowfoot. I thought nothing of half-drowning myself just to speak. I asked them, I wanted to know what it was that Remy took of me when he left, what did I have then that was now missing?

As an antidote to nightmare, Junior Lee from West Virginia, who couldn't have been more than five feet high and resembled the buffalo on the back of the American nickel, suggested flying. Not jumping off the roof into the wind's mad hands, nor sailing like Junior's wife Kitty, fuelled by Canadian Club, into the outer reaches of everyone's tolerance, but dreaming wings, unfurling them triumphantly as flags, soaring into the sky far above the reaching women and the stalking cat with its burnt-black paws expanding into the night.

I called to Remy and what came to me I didn't want. It wasn't what I meant by his name.

I knew about the difficulties of flight, the cost of weightlessness, the afflictions of creatures careening out of the sky suffering stage fright, lost nerve, shedding their intentions in a sudden shower. When my brother and I tried to levitate we stuck to the earth heavy as anchors. We didn't have to swallow stones for ballast, it seemed that's all we were. My father told us about a man who had rivulets of scars running down his back for having been airborne as a baby. An eagle had swooped down and snatched him off the ground where he'd been playing. The eagle, an intelligent bird, should have known better, should have resisted the impulse, as the mother was a crack shot and blasted off its head with her handy Remington, while the baby's sisters ran into the field, into a gentle storm of birdflesh and feathers, to catch their brother like a tumbling down cherub.

When Junior Lee was even smaller, a boy, he used to fly kites. He said his father warned him repeatedly to hold on tightly to the string, *Hold on, Junior, for God's sake!*, so that one day when the kite got caught in the propeller of a low-flying twin-engine airplane, he was lifted into the air, up over his father's head like a passing shadow. He landed in a tree about a mile away, stranded high in its branches, bruised and badly scratched, one arm dangling, but intending to stay put because he'd finally let go of the string and was afraid to come down.

When I was five, birds appeared to me as lightly dressed miracles. Though even they had bodies made real by accident or disease: lung worm, heart failure, broken wings, severed talons, slashed eyes. It makes you wonder. We have all this material wound around us, this long constricting scarf of skin. Taut across the belly, holding in a rushing red sea. And those women, those old grimalkins, how they enter through unknown channels – at some point in your life they'll speak only in madness. Don't be deceived about childhood. You can be five and know that something is about to be born, something scratching inside you, batting around your insides like a cat playing with your guts. All summer you can feel it growing, ripening in the heat. You will be delivered of yourself, you think, but this takes years.

Boats purr across the water, a blended hum of voices fills the camp. In the fall it empties into silence until the hunters arrive with their arsenal of punctuation, bringing the lyric of the lives they track to a full stop. Their lust is such that, dissolving into the bush, they sometimes take each other for quarry. That year, Abel Pogue, a veteran hunter, died in his sleep in Americana. His young grandson slept beside the body all night and in the morning would say only this, *I want his guns and his hat.* Doc Bailey, who went into the cabin to comfort the boy, came out shaking his head, disgusted, muttering, *That little bastard.*

Around this time I was taken to school, led by the hand to a place I didn't want to go, and left there. No amount of begging bought me my passage back home. No one came to rescue me, not even my grandfather who could usually be trusted in matters of rebellion and escape. I was powerless, as we all were. Even though our cheeks were still masked in babyfat, sorrow was plainly visible on them. Its damp imprint unmistakable, and yet this was taken no more seriously than the clouds boiling black and murderous above our parents' unprotected heads.

# *Visitation*

OH, IT WAS one of those glorious days. The wind swishing around outside warm as spit, the sun rubbing its huge buttery face against the windows. Urla was upstairs making the bed, flipping the sheets up and up catching bellyfuls of air, watching them settle, then *whoop* up again. Not the way you'd make a bed, I'm sure. Never mind, Urla had time – elastic minutes, double-decker hours, days long as the Lord's nose. She had time and she meant to spend it, splash it around, but *whoop* what was that? That shadow falling, like a leaf spiralling down, slipping the length of the sheers, slowly with a faint *hisss*.

Must investigate, Urla was like that, curious as a kid, so she marched around to the other side of the bed and *whoa*, hang on, it can't be. But it was. Crumpled, curled up foetal on the floor, charred to a crisp like something long forgotten on the barbecue: a devil. Just a small one mind you, peewee league, about the size of a squirrel or a Ken doll. But a devil most definitely with those tiny horns and shredded bat's wings and that spade-ended tail limp as a piece of burnt string.

Urla crossed herself, though she needn't have. The thing looked pathetic, really. Pain was etched claw-deep on its scorched face and its wee tongue lolled out pink as a kitten's (without that grimace, it might have been a downright handsome devil, too). Urla's heart, easily stoked, began to warm. *Poor creature.* She was tempted to touch it, give it an experimental pinch to see if it was still kicking. Devils are supposed to be immortal, aren't they? Urla sighed. What's the world coming to, she couldn't help but wonder, when this sort of thing starts dropping out of the sky like scat. Thank goodness she'd had the rug Scotchgarded. She supposed it might be a fallen angel, a stray Beelzebub, or some kamikaze fiend on an aborted mission. Divine mischief or debris, how can you tell? What did she know, anyway? Verne had been a hell-raiser all right, but as far as the real thing goes, go ask Gracie, her mother-in-law, she was a regular demonologist, knew all about devils and their devious ways. Religion! Her tongue wagged non-stop when she got on *that* subject. Not that she was talking to Urla any more. Nope, ever since Verne passed on, absolute silence (*praise be* for some things!).

Urla hunkered down for a better look. Her hand drifted forward, she was a tactile person, after all. 'Gol, Url,' her friends liked to tease, 'you'd hug just about anything.' Not that this little dickens here was all that tempting with its black reptilian skin. And, she had to consider, it might be carrying some deadly disease, might be crawling with infernal vermin. It might be radioactive, for goodness' sakes, or *rabid.* A co-worker, some satanic comrade, might have given it the fatal bite. She didn't imagine their hygiene was up to much down there. Nor their manners. Tempers would flare in that incinerating heat. Perhaps a dose of Lysol was in order, Urla thought, a light misting over the corpse. But was it dead or alive, she hadn't settled that question yet.

Urla cocked her head and let her ear hover over the devil like a space ship, zooming in close, hoping to pick up some signal, a muted psychic chatter, a whisper of evil. Nothing, not a sound. Though that smell, coiling around her face like steam, crawling up into her nostril, *phew* that took her back a decade or two. Hair oil, pimple cream, lemon gin, laid rubber – a malodorous concoction. Distilled in human form it could only add up to one thing, a teenage boy. Didn't Verne use to smell like that with her wrapped around him close as skin as they ripped up the back roads in his dad's car, two drinking kissing fools, *Christ* they had fun. He was crazy about her. Times he was just plain crazy. Like when she went out with Bud Lawson over to the show in Espanola and Verne followed them, got his hands around Bud's skinny neck in the drug store parking lot and she *screamed.* He loved her so much. Called her 'kitten' and 'cupcake' when they were first married. Boy, did that change. And fast. Before she knew it, she was getting 'cow' and 'elephant' and 'stupid bitch.' Then he started taking those swipes at her. Fooling around, a slap here, a kick there, like he was trying to knock the fat off her ass, trying to punch it back into her face the way you punch down bread dough.

Sure she put on some weight after losing the baby, it wasn't her fault. Talk about demonic, Verne had a mean streak in him, a wide ugly one that cut straight through his heart. Gracie couldn't see it, naturally. He was nearly perfect as far as she was concerned, so she set to work on Urla. *Why didn't Urla lose a few pounds, at least try to make herself pretty for him, a little will power (and prayer) was all it took, she'd be steadier on her feet for one thing, wouldn't keep falling down and bumping into things.* How else could she possibly be getting those black eyes and bruises the size of saucers floating up her arm? Urla let her see them too, she didn't try to hide anything. Gracie's no fool – she knew what was going on. Once she even confided to Urla that Verne was having a 'spiritual problem.' Wasn't that a good one, a real thigh-slapper. Yeah, he was having a spiritual problem and it came out of a bottle like a genie. Urla even knew its name, Captain Morgan, swashbuckling in, dressed to the nines, flashier than the Holy Ghost, just dying to hit her with a revelation.

That one night Verne came home, pissed to the gills as usual, and pulled her out of bed, dragged her down the stairs into the kitchen, she was still half-asleep, dreaming, hallucinating, something weird going on in her head to account for the enormous hands that suddenly appeared through the ceiling like the kind you see in old religious movies reaching down from heaven. Lovely hands, strong and fatherly, uncalloused, well-manicured, smelling of Old Spice, each one the size of a man. Amazing. Well maybe she was getting tipsy on that blood cocktail sliding down her throat, Verne ramming her head into the fridge, a vile mix of words spewing out of his mouth. The hands looked real enough, though, and when they fluttered open like wings Urla saw plain and simple that she was going to die. *This was it.* Verne had finally done it. These heavenly hooks had come to get her, to deliver her soul from the swollen bag of pain that was her body, to cradle it like a newborn child. She was ready too, she wanted to go. But you know what? She had it figured wrong. What did the monstrous hands do but begin to applaud Verne, urging him on, clapping thunderbolts, it was deafening. Then bedamned if they didn't ball up into fists and fall on Urla, pounding and pounding, driving her like a nail through the *jeezly* floor.

*Oh, why not*, she went ahead and placed a tentative finger on the devil, testing it the way you might a warming pot of soup. Somehow she didn't expect it to have such solidity – a cold sad fact. The tip of her finger retained a darkish smudge, like she'd been stubbing out butts in an ashtray.

Urla frowned. Her mind was working like a Singer trying to stitch this thing together. Fear didn't enter into it. She wasn't about to start screeching like some women she knew might. All the same, she hoped this wasn't the start of something, dishes leaping off the counter, poltergeists cleaving the curtains like buzzsaws. She had no intention of putting up with that kind of nonsense, *thank you very much.*

Disposal was obviously going to be a problem. How exactly did a person get rid of one of these anyway? Flush it down the toilet and you'd plug the works. Put it out with the garbage? Somehow that didn't seem right. Besides, somebody might find it, wouldn't that be a laugh? She could just pick it up by the tail like a dead rat and bury it in the garden. Sure, might as well pour in toxic waste. That'd be the end of her prize petunias.

*Why her*, was what Urla really wanted to know. It must mean something. She knew that meaning was attached like a price tag to most things. Might be some sort of omen. Might, and this thought suddenly elbowed its way into view, might be meant to make her feel guilty, stir up her conscience. *Hell*, if that was the case, let it rain devils, *let it pour.*

When Verne drowned himself was she sorry? Hardly, are you kidding? So she helped him along. That's what a good wife is for, right? To lend a helping hand. Right. So she placed that helping hand smack on his chest and pushed, *down*, way down into the water. He was having a bath. It was easy as pie, he was half-corked anyway. Didn't his eyes bug out, though? He must have been surprised. Urla could feel his heart leaping like a fish into her palm, faster and faster, then slower and slower. He was trying to say something to her but all that came out of his mouth were bubbles, sweet nothings, zeros – add them up and you had the sum total of all he'd ever said to her, really.

She baptized him all right. Gave him a whole new life, somewhere else. He should be grateful. She was.

Naturally the police asked a few questions about the accident. People weren't blind; they could figure it out for themselves. They knew Urla had already served a life sentence. She'd done her time.

*And you'd better believe it,* Urla thought, finally gathering the cindery Lucifer into her arms and rising up, her old knees cracking, she'd work it out, she'd manage. It was like anything else in life, wasn't it? A person simply found a place for things like this. They made them fit.

*Amen.*

# Two Bastards

IF YOU WERE to reach into the past, sorting through images as through a pile of old photographs, you might see a young woman wearing a wedding dress running through the snow, diamonds of ice tumbling into her boots. You might see her as a girl diving off the town dock, playful as an otter in the lake, or older, a woman marching through town carrying a flag, a ribbon of children leaping and twirling behind her. Someone might say, 'Oh, that's Jane Pecore, Johnny Pecore's mother. On Armistice Day 1918, she walked into Cruther's drug store and bought a Union Jack, then marched up and down every street in town, flag held high, while the church bells rang and rang, and the boat whistles blew. Everything that could make a noise did and kept it up.'

That's not her then, you think, and continue searching, sifting again through images, fragments of time shuffled and stacked like a deck of cards. You see the *Emerald* from Wikwemikong sailing into the bay with a brass band playing on the hurricane deck. You see a man highwire on the peak of a barn – raving. The *E.U. Jennie* struck by lightning, the Ocean House in flames. You see familiar faces, distant visual echoes of people you know. A young Mackie with fine features, that would be Horace, his family line as yet untouched by the eventual marriage into the Stalker clan. Others crowd into view. Charlie Waundabence, who delivered the first letter to Sheguiandah. Abe Lusk, a man dogged by premonition. One morning, in the new century, he woke to the sound of his Spider Island cottage being ripped and crushed by something looming large outside.

But you don't see Finn – he's what you might call a deep-water man – just as you don't see photographs of the dead. Or of a man grieving, his head buried in the shoulder of a woman. You don't see him, but you see her. Finally.

She isn't running or diving or marching, but sitting quietly, biding her time, and yours. Small and prim, expressionless, emotion if any completely contained. Not what you were expecting. Though that's how she carried it off: she was never what anyone was expecting. Nothing about her snags your attention, stops your eye. Her looks are plain, her dress is modest and buttoned to the neck (buttons *not* pearl). On her feet, tiny narrow shoes, the kind you sometimes see in museums with people staring at them, astonished, wondering *how on earth* as they shift their own ugly-sister-sized feet restlessly. Witch's shoes, that seem to support a notion of the past as being cribbed, confining, full of dust falling thick as a pelt on everything. Clouds of dust probably are billowing on the street outside her house, churned up by a clatter of horse-drawn wagons, though the room in which she sits has clear air and polished surfaces. There's no dust on her, either. Never mind this calm you've caught her in, she's a busy woman. Busy marshalling family and household, not to mention her work for the church, her social activities, and her other involvements – with the illicit and the depraved.

Suddenly she rises, breaking the teasing anonymity with her name. Helen Frances Crawford Cullis. It rolls out easily as a patterned runner for anyone to use. She's 'Helen' to her husband, Byron T. Cullis, a lawyer who addresses everyone accusingly. 'Fran' and 'Cissy' to her friends, the respectable ones, and 'Cristy' to Finn, who thought that name suited her better. He thought it captured more of her unusual light. Finn was fond of light: moonbeams, sunbeams, any play of light upon the water. Probably because he lived in the dark like a rat in a hole. She has other names as well, secret ones, and silly forgotten nicknames that her poor fond mother gave her. Her father never called her anything. He buggered off for good the day she was born. Out of wedlock, as it was called, though she soon learned other less lyrical terms for who she was. 'Norah's Little Bastard' was a name she wore like a dirty dress until she finally ducked it, left it floating on a fetid pool somewhere in the south. After that she accumulated names quickly and hoarded them like wealth. A range of names, she found, made life more interesting, the same as having a second language. A fluency that brought her the unexpected. Like Finn.

He couldn't believe her eyes. They were the colour of island shale and the hardest he'd ever seen. Murderer's eyes, devil's eyes, harder than that, he couldn't believe it.

She could nail a man to the floor with a look, and did.

Compassion, you realize, doesn't concern her. At least she doesn't practise it, the kind of seeing that slops over onto things, blurring distinctions. Her eye, honed by survival, is sharp. She can pick the invisible out of the sky, read insect scrawl, what the leaves write in the air when the wind tears them out of the trees. How else would she know that Finn was coming? He could hardly communicate by any legitimate means. Send her a letter from Owen Sound or Quebec City or wherever the hell he was, telling her that he'd be there in a week's, a month's time: *Dearest C. Crossing October 24. Be at Ocean House. Midnight. Finn.* No, it could only come cryptically. A sign so slight as to be almost overlooked, or an omen unmistakable and unforgettable. A glass exploding in her hand at dinner, a pair of snakes copulating on the doorstep, a laughing gull dropping a loose white bundle of shit on Byron's bowler hat, fastidiously dusted only moments before. (This happened frequently enough that he was soon to offer his sons a penny for every dead gull, laughing or otherwise, they produced.) She became adept at divining, at drawing significance out of the ground, out of the water, at cracking open codes like seeds and watching them unfurl like wildflowers blossoming. She's literate as an animal with an elemental script. She has those eyes like stones that break into things – looking for Finn. She might appear frail and childlike, subject to vapours, but she can stare a path through the seething scum in any turn-of-the-century barroom and find him.

She's worth watching, then. Once she starts to move beauty kindles her.

Pacing the room, now standing by the window, she raises a hand and lifts the lace curtain. Looks out. The Cullis home, a mansion by local standards, is situated on a hill that overlooks the town.

It's flanked by a few other Victorian houses which together contain most of the town's elite, such as it is: a doctor, an Anglican Church minister, a couple of merchants, the owner of a sawmill, their wives and children. So she gazes down from a certain height. What she sees has a different and more attractive character than it will possess years later. A rough port town, randy with energy, populated mainly by a shifting drifting body of strangers – sailors, lumberjacks, salesmen, gamblers, even the odd tourist. The clashing commerce of their lives creates a beguiling confusion easy enough to enter into unnoticed. If you lived in one of those grand houses on the hill, you could slip out quick as a shadow late at night, leaving sons and husband strangling gulls in their sleep, dreaming of fortunes. You could slide behind trees and banks and unhitched wagons, the moon your only witness. You could enter an alley like a cat, meet a man with no name, speak any kind of violence. You could do this if you were a woman like her, drawn to the disreputable as the Irish are said to be drawn to rivers, the place where poetry is revealed to them. And it may be so in her case, she might well be compelled by an unseemly and debased verse twisting serpentine in the streets below. The other women in her social circle, Justine Trimbell or Elizabeth Vincent, would not have paused in the middle of the day like this. Utterly loyal to the tea service and the silverware, to the prosaic safety of their homes, they would not have wandered even in thought to where a rat might skitter by, scrawling its devilish long signature in the dirt. But for her by the window, fierce eyes locked on something escaping her down the street along the dock, there's no telling where exactly her loyalty is located, or where, like a skittish kind of light, it might settle next.

Finn's fidelities were another matter. He lived on the water, came ashore only when he had to, and never so far inland that he couldn't hear the lake talking. He loved its soft singing voice, its fanciful endearments and revelations. *Finn, dear boy,* it crooned, *you're a shark-souled creature, eel-dark you are, though your heart is a fluttering sunfish. Be careful on land, Finn, it's a treacherous place, your father died there. He was a kelpie, your mother a storm.* In truth, Finn had no parents, or none that could be traced. He was a foundling, discovered in a bucket on board the *Asia.* Only two weeks old and as good as dead until the cook, Flossie Strain, warmed him in her rough red onion-scented hands and fed him a mixture of rum and fish broth. He was passed around and raised on all the steamers that travelled the lakes then, both the Black Line and the White Line: the *Pacific,* the *Athabaska,* the *Waubuno,* the *Majestic,* the *Evangeline,* the *North Wind.* These boats gave him countless sailor fathers and the occasional mother, though no parent as generous as the water itself. It could provide almost anything in a practical or spiritual line: bass for supper, mirages for entertainment, theology and lore, mischief to keep you on your toes, grief certainly, if that was your particular need. And commentary. Like dreaming, its voice flowed endlessly in and out of awareness. Most ignored it or talked over it, but Finn was an attentive listener and picked up a bible's-worth of information. He knew every shoal, star and omen, every creature that lurked above and below the waterline. He knew the unmistakable smell of death on a doomed ship and had gained a reputation for foresight and magic. It was said he could control the wind at will. Other men feared him and so granted him more power that he actually possessed. Like a dangerous rock in the bay, he developed a certain tale-gathering property; stories caught like night around him. Nor did he discourage them. He was solitary by nature, and silent, and dressed always in black like a man involved with mystery. At times he affected a brooding brutish look that kept everyone at a distance. He had a gold tooth, a gold earring, and wore around his neck a silver bosun's call that was shaped like a dog's penis. His body was an aviary of bird tattoos: a hawk on one wrist, a bracelet of finches on the other, ducks on each foot to keep him from drowning, an eagle circling his solar plexus, bluebirds rising over his shoulder landing down his back, and a large lacy-winged crow spanning his ass like a pair of fancy French pants.

Finn's virtues led a devious sort of existence, which served him well with Cristy. She appreciated the furtiveness involved. She liked to find the good in him, scaring it to the surface so that she could better abuse it. Most of the men the pandering lake brought her were easy to figure, whatever they had to offer straightforward as a black eye or a broken jaw. Not Finn. He was a puzzle in which brutality and sensitivity fit together.

This is how they met: I was out, she says, late as usual. Two men were waiting for me, one at the Queen's, the other at the Huron, and both of them tensed for trouble like cocked guns. Let them wait, I thought, and strolled down by the dock. It was a beautiful night, clear and warm, moonlight on everything. I saw something, I didn't know what, curled up under a bush by the water's edge. A huge shadowy lump of a thing. Dead or alive, I couldn't guess. But I had to know, I'm like that, so I walked over and gave it a kick, a real dandy, I have these sharp little shoes. Well, Finn says, I thought a bloody knife was entering my side. I thought I was being murdered there on the shore, and me half-asleep, and the sparrows wedged in the bush above me burst out of their dreams like bullets. I rolled and sprang and got her by the throat, her pulsing white throat, I couldn't believe what I had in my hands. One of those well-bred church-going women you never get to touch because they're tethered like angels to their husbands and their homes. Yet here was one drifting loose, free as sin. And I had her by the throat, my greasy black nails digging in. You know, she didn't scream or anything. That amazed me, how she just stood there calm as the night taking me apart piece by piece with her eyes. I dropped my hands and said, *Ma'am, what can I do for you?* and she said, well, I won't tell you what she said, I couldn't believe that either. Though I tried to accommodate her as best I could, and I must say we had a good time.

To her, Finn is like an enchanted island. He appears and disappears. He hides behind trees, behind rocks, he steps out of the fog to grab her, he vanishes in the mist. He'll steam in on one boat then leave almost immediately on another. He'll wave to her from the dock, saluting her with a gesture meant, she supposes, as some sort of worship. He's being ironic, of course. Sometimes he stays around for weeks, suffering land sickness the way some people suffer on the water. If it's too cold to live outside he takes a room in one of the hotels and she scales the fire escape, a rickety ladder nailed on the back wall, and climbs through his window. Once she climbed into the wrong room but stayed anyway, sleeping with that man instead. She hadn't seen Finn for months. He was gone the next morning. Another time, slipping into his room she saw three women surging on the bed around him. She smiled, that little smile like a curved pike's bone, and he told the women to go. He called them names and so did she. They sat on the bed together watching the women dress, laughing, competing, seeing who could be more crude.

Finn and Cristy. Baiting one another, teasing mercilessly like brother and sister. Meeting her after a long absence he might say, *Bloody hell: you again?* and earn for himself a cold hand across his face and a back view of her, a controlled and tidy fury flying down the stairs, when what he longed for more than anything was Cristy close as breath. Theirs was a lively game that took nerve and skill, like playing catch with knives. They bluffed each other crazy, one outdoing the other. What marriage, moderate and cramped, decayed with dependency, could have withstood it? Such a union they would have destroyed easily and happily like that room they set fire to in the Ocean House.

As it was, he could always leave and she could always wait. Though not helplessly, not like a woman who wasn't master of the situation. He pays. He pays for everything, even his pain. Times she refuses to see him – he's just not there. He's like that, enchanted, fading to nothing, and at least half the sorcery is hers.

She might be thinking of this as she stands by the window, her wealth of names draped around her. Though the woman with light falling into her hands spilling over onto her dress is simply Cristy. Finn's Cristy. No last name.

Her focus has shifted upward. She's searching the sky now, for a message perhaps from him. Perhaps it's been years. The final bluff stretching further than the lake itself. The sky is strangely empty, not a bird in sight. Finn told her that the absence of birds around a ship is a bad sign; stars too near, phosphorescence in the water, singing or bells tolling below are all portents of trouble. He had, *has* she corrects, funny beliefs.

A story of his: A woman one day while walking along the shore came across the body of a drowned man. As there was no one to see her, she robbed the body, taking the man's gold ring, gold coins from his pocket, and his watch (a silver Waltham). That night a bird appeared at her bedroom window, shrieking and beating against the glass. She couldn't discourage it, couldn't drive it away, couldn't kill it. It was deathless and relentless, returning night after night, keening and crashing against her window, until finally the woman went mad.

Some elements in this story changed from one telling to the next, it might be a man robbing a woman, but it always ended in madness. Finn liked that.

Cristy used to look out this window and see the most amazing things. A blood-coloured sky, a murder of crows dragging night out of the bushes, a winking conspiratorial moon, shuddering planets and stars. 'One time,' she says out loud, 'I saw a boat with black sails floating above the treetops, the crew themselves dressed dark as thunder, and I knew then, sure as a warm stirring wind brings a storm, that he was coming.'

She glances aside, mouth twisted into a smile, cat-sly eyes aimed at us in the meddling future, as if to say, *You fools, you'll believe anything, won't you?*

Helen Cullis. She made you turn, made you look at her, and now, like an unknowable subject in an old evocative photograph, she intends to keep the best secrets to herself. Nothing you can do. She takes her life, just like that, and stops it. Lets the past snake through her fingers, disabling her hand, the way Finn once did clutching it so hard she wanted to cry.

## Public Mischief

PAPA McFATRIDGE had one vice, alcohol; one talent, making money; and four virtues – Janine, Lucille, Georgiana, and Frances, known as Frank. This particular combination eventually killed him. As his liver and wallet were of equal size when he died, he was able to leave the virtues, his daughters, in comfortable circumstances – at least from his point of view, which at the reading of the will was cupid-height. Gathered in the manager's office of the Belvedere Hotel, his 'girls' discovered they were about to be married. To dust-haunted corridors, to hundreds of soiled unmade beds, to miles of smudged sweat-smeared glass. To the usual thing, that is: work.

McFatridge had left one of his four hotels to each. Confident in his reading of each child's character – four chapters in his own life after all – he provided them each with an ideal match in brick and mortar, forgetting that in marriage compatibility is seldom the point. This accomplished, he slipped through a crack in the wall and floated upward like an exhaled puff of stale air. Good thing he'd never gotten around to fixing that crack. Through it he escaped the sour looks of his daughters, who were more disposed to courtship than ownership, and ascended into general dissipation, consorting with the turbulent currents travelling far above and away from the city.

Janine, the eldest and tallest, found herself saddled with the Belvedere, the oldest and most respectable hotel. It was an appealing place, but had definitely seen better days. It had once housed the eminent in their brief passage through town – fragile or robust vessels of political fervour, artistic virtuosity, or royal blood. Its hardwood had felt the waltzing feet of Baron Renfrew, later king. A century ago the Emperor of Brazil and his retinue occupied a whole floor for three days, their monkeys skittering up the coiled ropes that served as fire escapes in each of the rooms. It was here in the twenties that a famous and temperamental baseball player had run amok, smashing chandeliers with his equally famous bat.

Four hundred thousand fawn bricks rising four stories into pediment and cornice, the Belvedere was considered an architectural gem, and Janine herself was beginning to feel the same. She was thirty-four, and time was rounding on her, pecking away, stealing bits of colour out of her hair and skin. The widow's peak that cut her face into a valentine now chased love away, pointing like a claw at subtle changes: frown lines lightly but indelibly etched on her forehead; eyes that were sharper, more calculating, as if watching from a greater distance; and a smile that was less pliant, less sympathetic than it once had been. Janine bore her mother's name, and much of her burden as well. Mama McFatridge had loaded it on her daughter's back like a picnic lunch before running off with a man who claimed to be the inventor of the curve ball. Some picnic. It had the weight of rocks. Papa didn't notice, as he was on a bender at the time, staggering from one hotel to the next (you could hardly refuse the owner a drink). He collapsed at the Harp, where the girls dragged him upstairs to an empty room. How could he miss Mama, he was seeing double and felt himself surrounded by women. He always wondered at such moments why an excess of yin in the universe had to be vented in *his* household. When he finally sobered up and realized that Mama was gone, the only thing that really bothered him, that kept him awake at nights, was the worry that his wife, somewhere in the world, was producing for some bastard a *son*.

Though as son substitutes go, Papa had no complaint with Janine. She *was* tall. To her a hug usually meant that she would have to study, once again, the tender, crooked, and obscenely white part in some man's hair. She was born rangy, arms and legs flailing angrily, and grew fast. Growing wasn't a clandestine activity with her as it was with most children, done in the dark at night. She flaunted it, shooting up rudely before startled adult eyes, then sticking out her tongue. When Georgiana was a baby and that dog ran off with her down the street, Janine was the one who caught up to it in half a dozen long strides and kicked the poor brute until it let go. You could do worse than have a daughter like Janine.

You could have a daughter like Lucille. She got the Royal Hotel and instantly changed its name to the Cadillac. Her sisters wondered what she would do for crockery, given her volatility. First the dishes went. Next, the help. When John McDougall, former light-heavyweight boxing champion and Royal bartender for twenty-seven years, heard that Lucille had inherited it, he packed his bags and headed south. 'For the good of my health,' he said.

To the unsuspecting, though, Lucille was a dream. To look at, to touch, hair glowing like moonlight around her lucent face, eyes the colour of nightshade. But in her head she kept stoked a glowing bed of embers, and on her person – a ferret. More than one guest would stumble down to breakfast in the morning with tiny bites pocking their body as if gnawed on during the night by an elf.

The only person who trusted Lucille was Georgiana, and she'd had a few shingles shaken loose during that incident with the dog. Georgiana was fey and near-sighted, and her connections with the world of commerce were tenuous. So she was willed the Harp, a sturdy little hotel downwind from the newly christened Cadillac, with an off-key piano and a yawning, yarning barroom clientele. Here, too much drink produced a volume of stories, rather than something that had to be sluiced off the floor. Barrels of beer translated directly into the meandering and soporific. You might step into the Harp late of an afternoon and find a snoring symphony; heads slumped or propped against the wall, or cradled in the crooks of arms like eggs in nests. It was the main function of the Harp's bouncer, Ed Ratti, to act as nurse-maid, to see that everyone was tucked up comfortably. He fussed and coddled, patting heads and chucking chins, making sure his charges were safe from drafts and nasty cricks-in-the-neck. When their wives and girl-friends stopped by at five o'clock, Ed delivered them, dazed and red-eyed, speechless now, into caring and careworn hands.

When Georgiana moved in with Ed Ratti, right into his room that is, her sisters were dismayed. They reasoned that perhaps she still needed nurturing and protection. Only Lucille saw it as a shrewd move and suspected her simple sister of having the whiphand after all. She kept this insight to herself, like most things, being indebted to Georgiana for the unwisely invested trust. Whether Georgiana had her wits about her or not, she kept up appearances, her dottiness enhanced now by the fiery tongues of fur that clung to her clothes, compliments of Tiger the barcat.

Tiger was a former resident of the Flying Horse, known among the locals as the 'Flying Tables and Chairs'. It went to the baby, nineteen-year-old Frank. Papa must have thought that the pent-up and unsettled atmosphere of the Horse needed Frank's 'feminine touch', the persuasive force of which had been furthered by weight training. She would beguile the rowdies, or else knock them silly. While the Belvedere had character, the Flying Horse had a reputation. If someone was going to be stabbed or shot in the city, it usually happened here, where menace and desire and inspiration came to a head, a dangerous fomenting brew. Frank felt it the moment she walked through the front door, passing Tiger on his way out.

The cat was sick to death of being pissed on – a direct hit won a free round at the Horse – and he'd had it with the Beauregard sisters upstairs and Hi Henry the dancing bellhop. They rubbed his fur the wrong way, pulled his whiskers, dropped him down the stairwell. They were *no different, no better* than the living.

So, fur spiked with urine and reeking, Tiger passed Frank at the door as she was moving in. He followed a pair of shiny Florsheims which crossed the street and stepped smartly into the Harp. There he was gathered into the massive tattooed arms of Ed Ratti, who gave him a nice bath and a bowlful of milk –

Tiger's first unalcoholic beverage – and a warm bed on a woman's crimson skirt that smelled of vanilla and cloves, and something indefinable to Tiger, which was grass.

LISTING THE HOTELS with real estate simply wasn't an option. To the McFatridges this would have been like dragging tiresome new husbands off to a slave market. Besides, the Belvedere was the family home. They'd been weaned in its bar on Shirley Temples (with just a touch of gin), and they'd had their tonsils taken out on the long lobby table by an itinerant doctor. Spaciousness and choice were a balm to family relations. They had never quarrelled over sharing rooms, as there were plenty of those, and rarely fussed about food, since they simply chose what they wanted from the dining-room menu. Life, as they imagined it unfolding in ordinary houses in unbearably small rooms, had to be a grim affair. *Where* in a house, they wondered, did a child pursued by an enraged belt-wielding adult hide? Houses surely weren't safe for children. But hotels were magic.

One time little Frank went missing for days during a game of hide-and-seek. She was at length discovered in Miss Ritchie's third-floor room eating box after box of chocolates and listening, entranced, to the *facts of life* as understood by her generous hostess.

'Babies arrive when they want to,' Miss Ritchie informed her, 'usually on trains late at night. They are resourceful creatures and have no trouble getting here, but do you know, they often end up with the wrong parents. Spiteful people who pinch them and make them cry.'

Frank was amused. They had a high old time of it, ducking into closets or sliding under the bed when footsteps were heard along the corridor. Miss Ritchie always wanted a child, and now had one. A product of her own childlike ingenuity.

Hotel life was theatre and the girls knew from an early age that they were an essential part of the performance. They wore pretty dresses, giggled, and zoomed around like premature Graces, understudies for roles involving the dispensation of delight.

Their father's business sense and their mother's dramatic timing combined in them to produce entertaining opportunists. Janine would recite passages from Shakespeare to guests gathered in the sitting room after dinner. Ophelia's mad scene was the most lucrative. Frank would sing 'How Much Is That Doggie in the Window', and 'All I Want for Christmas Is My Two Front Teeth', with such a coy spin that hearts ached and hands dug deeply into purses. All Frank really wanted for Christmas was a cap gun and a tank which she was then able to buy for herself.

Georgiana had her own repertoire of effects. She could make her nose bleed on cue, a spurting scarlet stream that appeared along with tears if some kid looked at her the wrong way. Nothing gets more action than blood on a white dress, or a bright smear of it across the face. The kid's panicking parents would apply handkerchiefs, science, and affection. Of course, nothing stopped the flow like a fifty-cent piece slipped into Georgiana's trembling hand. This she would eventually lose to Lucille, who followed her sister like a hawk if she jingled.

Lucille could turn a profit playing poker or doing card tricks, but she seldom took the trouble. It was much easier to pick pockets, or, using a duplicate set of keys, comb through the guests' rooms when they were out. At eleven, already an accomplished thief, she often sat smoking on the roof of the Belvedere, contemplating her future, flicking butts into the street below, hoping to set some woman's hat on fire.

Lucille's envisioned future contained palm trees, casinos, slinky black dresses, heat, and motion. Mink slipped off her shoulder, silk slithered up her leg, strangers' hands rode the whole length of her body. It was life lived on the edge, on the wing, in the element of excitement, perpetually unfolding. She would gamble everything. Even her skin.

But when Lucille's present collided with her future – rammed it – time fused and sank in heaviness. Sure she wore fur, but it was yellow, with pink eyes, had a vicious bite and fleas. Motion played mostly on the limbs of her employees who walked out the door in a steady stream. They were fools, she felt, for taking her stinging words to heart. Only Clive, the desk clerk, smiled back at her when she fired him. No matter how she pitched her voice, low and hard, or shrill and searing, he took it as a joke, some kind of intuitive homage to *his* dreams, the ones closest to the surface of his life, wherein he was a lover to a woman all smoke and sparks. His tongue a licking red flame. Clive, the arsonist.

Janine got wind of it directly as Lucille's former help blew in the back door of the Belvedere, simpering or frothing, conjured into storms by her sister's hand, by her cheating and bluffing, her reneging on pay. And by her *bloody* ferret that got into everything, that fouled the linen and stole cigarettes (which it ate), that dragged away Mike Love's chihuahua, also named Mike, and chewed off its ears. Janine would stoop to listen, nodding over their anger like a canny mother using consolation as ointment, then she'd riffle-shuffle the deck, placing them next in the Harp or the Flying Horse. Once in the web of the sisters' employ, people found it difficult to escape.

Not that many wanted or needed to, discovering much in the compass of the four hotels that they liked. If growing up, growing old, meant surrendering pleasures, then that wasn't expected here. You did your job, then afterwards could gamble your pay at the Belvedere, or get smashed at the Cadillac, or float high on words at the Harp, where every night Mary Stinchcombe, the upstairs maid, hammered away on the piano providing a sub-melodic drive to the tallest of tales. Belief in them was optional. Belief in anything, possible. Not that there was much choice for anyone who worked at the Flying Horse, where the Beauregards sashayed from room to room, and Hi Henry slew-footed like ball lightning down the halls.

Mary Stinchcombe knew she was in the right place. She was aflame, kindled since she'd come from the Cadillac into this love nest, Georgiana and Ed Ratti generating an infectious heat. She had her eye on Harold, the new waiter, and had been tantalizing him with her musical prowess. Clearing the tables at midnight, he walked over to her at the piano, hands raised protectively to his ears, and grunted, '*Creeping Jesus,* give us a break, Mary.'

What she gave him was such a look that he backpedalled into a clustered family of chairs and fell among them.

What Mary daydreamed about, Tiger watched. After the bar closed at night, he followed Georgiana and Ed to their room, and leapt onto the dresser – best seat in the house. He pawed at a tangled snarl of doily and stockings and suspenders before settling down to observe:

some kind of language

language, though not sound entering words making connections in the air, the electric wiring of spoken lines

something more immediate, the tongue delivering its message directly to an arching foot, a calf, the inner thigh, labia

backs talked, legs circled, hands to nipples to hair, each finger a different dialect trilling down the spine

(his thumb fit exactly into her heartspoon)

two bodies, one white as teeth, one blue with ink, became a soliloquy

an argument, an appeasement

nothing to do with caterwauling in the alley

something newly born, raw

language ripped out of its skin

Tiger had seen people do a great many things to one another in the rooms of the Flying Horse, but never this.

While her sister conversed laterally and vertically with Ed Ratti, Janine would lie in the dark, alone, her hands folded beneath her like gloves. Once or twice she'd get up to switch on the light, sensing some other presence in the room, and loneliness would spring at her off bed sheets blank as paper. Her palms ached. With longing, with neuritis, she didn't see that it mattered what. The hotel creaked as if in sympathy when she turned off the light again and dumped herself back on the bed like a tired old suit.

Grievances ran through her head. Lucille. *Short* men. Parents. Thank goodness her own children were safe inside her, clasped in two tiny sacs – they rattled like dice. Why spill them out and feed them to the dark? She thought of Mary Stinchcombe over at the Harp, how she was throwing herself at that new waiter. That one. He'd gotten off the train and took that job at the Harp during the stopover, planning to get back on in half an hour. Ed caught him hurrying down the street with the ten-dollar float, a trayful of tips and five glasses of draft. *Son,* Ed had said, clamping an enormous arm around Harold's shoulder, *we don't see travel in your future.* What *did* they see, Janine wondered, that oddball trinity at the Harp, pooling their vision? It didn't take a cat's keen eye to see a long line of diapers. Mind you, in bed short men weren't too bad – if they could resist digging their toenails into your shins. *Sleep,* she said, like she was calling a dog, but the bugger wouldn't come.

The Beauregards never slept. They no longer required sleep's sweet replenishment. Past death, they were at their palest and loveliest, daughters of the south gliding ladylike without a whisper through walls. At night they kept watch. They made certain that Rosie the fortuneteller in room 19 was snoring soundly, communing with her agents. And that Noreen down the hall was being treated properly by her gentlemen callers. The Beauregards were severe when it came to manners and felt it their duty to let fall a burning candle or a fieldstone doorstop on a man's private parts should he act boorishly.

Illusions themselves, the sisters were nonetheless accustomed to creature comforts and drawn to flesh-and-blood excitements.

Which is why they had settled in the Flying Horse, northern headquarters at one time of Confederate spies and refugees. Ben Butler himself could harry them here to no avail – they would not be routed from their chosen afterlife. They'd stomp their little silk-clad feet, refusing to fly from him this time as they had many years before when his troops took New Orleans. Let him show his ugly Yankee mug and they'd wither him to a cinder with language they'd picked up in the bar over the years, drawling it like fire from a dragon's scarlet mouth.

The Beauregards' anger added a certain crackle to the already disturbed ambience of the Horse. The regulars and drunks loved them, apparitions in a smoke-filled room, muses of violence. They jumpstarted fights with simple tricks. Yanking a chair out from under someone, pouring beer in someone else's lap. And they kept at it, stirring things up until low comedy spiralled into rage. By the time noses were being broken and furniture was crumpling like stage props against the wall, they would be gone, vanished, having slipped into their invisibility as into a soft southern night.

In the morning, sun only hitting the walls, Frank would sweep up the broken glass and knock the tables and chairs back together. Mouth full of nails, she fondly surveyed the room – a home it seemed for disabled appointments – nothing matched any more, everything wobbled and squeaked. The clock above the bar had one lame hand that dragged itself around the dial, dismissing minutes, hours.

No one who frequented the Horse had much use for the time anyway. Frank figured she must know every undesirable in town by now. Nights here she felt like an apprentice roughrider struggling to bridle the kicking snorting beast they called up. But she was learning. She could read trouble in the way a crowd moved, in the rise and fall of conversation, and she knew who carried knives, who had sawed-off shotguns or wooden bats wrapped with electrical tape hidden in their coats. A wink to Bert behind the bar and he'd begin diluting drinks with water. Or if, out of the coarse weave of sound Frank picked up, 'Fucken wop, gonna hafta cut 'em up,' she'd prescribe a free round stiff enough to wire the guy to his chair.

Drunks confused speaking with thinking and Frank caught them out blathering in boozetalk, an inflated tongue, florid and sentimental, or purely vile, that staggered stupidly around its subject. She could bounce them out if she had to, though the one thing they held festering in their minds was a grudge. If murder were building to a theme, she might even alert the cops, who were on the payroll anyway and stopped by regular as cleaning staff. Once they arrived to find a man, who had been robbed and beaten, under a table in the arms of his assailant, both so drunk that speech had been driven out of their mouths up into their furious staring eyes.

What surprised Frank, no, what *astonished* her, was that she actually loved this place. Really loved it. That in this arranged match she had fallen head over heels. Like Hi Henry reworking his death on the stairs, trying to get it right, dancing down with a tray of glasses balanced on his head, his toe forever snagging that loop of frayed carpet. That was Frank, exactly, plunging into an intensity of emotion that might have frightened her if she weren't a rocksteady McFatridge, a virtue well grounded in earthly matters.

A pile of lumber risen foursquare, dressed with sills and sashes, would not infatuate many, but to Frank her hotel was alive, as dashing and desirable as any hero. She liked its seediness, its dark dirty corners, its rakishly torn wallpaper, the fitchy smell of the rooms. Even the stale repulsive odour of beer and smoke that hung permanently in the bar did not, by some alchemy of affection, put her off. She listened closely to its whispering skirring voice as mice ran their nightlong steeplechase behind the baseboards, and she laughed aloud, as if at a practical joke, when firebrats sprang out of her hair in the morning.

Maybe she was as loony as Georgiana. The thought had occurred to her. But then, placing her hand on the warm sunlit wall seeking response, a pulse, she'd think, *I'll never leave you.* A thrill played on her spine and made her shudder, but it was only Hi Henry taking a shortcut through her, pausing just long enough for her to feel him, a cool waterfall of pleasure tumbling from her head down.

THE FIRST TIME Clive slid his arms around Lucille, he found himself staring eyeball to eyeball with the ferret. The first time she knocked him off his feet, she used a bowling ball, having been a terror to the pinboys in the local bowling alley when she was growing up. He dropped a firecracker down the back of her dress. She replied with a butcher knife that shaved a tick of flesh off his ear before shattering a picture on the wall behind – a photograph of Papa shaking hands with a jolly Rotarian (a doctor eventually charged with poisoning several of his patients). Lucille followed up the butcher knife with an antique comb-back rocker that was colonized by termites and folded like lawn furniture on impact. This annoyed her particularly as she had stolen it from the Belvedere and expected better quality. She had a good mind to complain, but had to keep an eye on Clive, who was keeping an eye on her.

Just as well, for Janine was already fuming. If Frank had gone queer over her hotel, refusing to pass through its doors, then it seemed Lucille was determined to drive hers down a rathole into bankruptcy. (Not that money was a problem for her as long as she could pry open the Harp's till.) Who would work at the Cadillac now? Janine would soon have to resort to blackmail or conscription. And if some clueless joker wandered in off the street wanting a room for the night, he'd be hard pressed to find Clive – who would be upstairs stalking Lucille, and she busy devising some ingenious ambush. The place was a mess. Beds trashed, garbage in the halls, every window on the second floor broken, this from a war game in which one of them was armed with billiard balls, the other a sack of potatoes. Even the ferret had limped into hiding with a broken paw.

Words meant absolutely nothing to Clive. Not that he couldn't comprehend or speak them – they simply had no power over him. Beautiful words failed to move him. Sharp words failed to wound, funny words to amuse. Lucille experimented, airing the exquisite in one breath, the odious in the next. Language both sprightly and dead, poetic flights and base slang, all with the same effect. Call him *darling* or *dickhead*, he didn't care. The only time she ever saw him reading a book, there was smoke billowing out of it – he'd been playing with matches. And yet he fascinated her. How he picked the wings off words, squeezed the very life out of them.

In twilight, they would sit together on the floor of the lobby, weary after hacking the day to bits. The hotel would be quiet as a church, nighthawks crying in the street outside, bats opening like black buds in the rafters far above them. It was then that Lucille would speak to Clive, words pointed right at him, or dipping and swerving. His expression never varied. But he watched her intently, a dark scribble of hair fallen onto his forehead, while he sucked one of her fingers or chewed on the hem of her dress.

THE DAY of the wedding, Baby Harold was after Tiger. As usual, there was the problem of Mary Stinchcombe, the thick layer of her that Baby had to sock his fist into to get the cat's attention. Baby, *in utero*, would punch and Tiger would bat at the sudden leaping knot of flesh, like a mouse trying to break through Mary's skin. But Tiger had grown tired of the game and had wandered off to caper on the wedding cake. Baby Harold blamed his mother. He whaled away at her, making the satin stretched tight across her belly pucker and buckle.

The wedding was to have taken place at two o'clock in the bar of the Belvedere. In preparation, waiters had whisked glasses away from patrons and covered the tables with white linen and vases full of flowers and weeds that Georgiana had gathered in backlots that morning. Shortly before two, Mary Stinchcombe burst through the Ladies and Escorts door on the arm of Ed Ratti and waddled up the aisle. Or rather, blazed a trail, as chairs had to be quickly pushed aside and an aisle improvised. Janine had turfed old Reverend Neary out of his room at the Harp and had propped him up against the bar, which was to serve as an altar, bottles standing stiff as saints behind him.

Everything was ready, everyone waiting. Even the Beauregard sisters had settled like veils of mist in the honeymoon suite of the Flying Horse, keenly anxious for the arrival of the happy couple. Frank's bartender, Bert, had received a little extra in his paycheque to perform the duties of Best Man. He didn't know then, of course, that he would spend the whole afternoon scouring the town for the missing groom.

Harold didn't show.

Lucille was the only one who looked pleased.

Frank, at once lovesick and homesick for the Horse, suggested a round of drinks. Everyone cheered and rallied to the call. Before long, Baby Harold was being lulled to sleep by a tide of alcohol rinsing through the amniotic sac, and by the rising voices that spun a soft cocoon of sound around his mother. Mary leaked colostrum onto the front of her wedding dress.

At five o'clock the Gentlemen Only door creaked open and a roomful of flushed faces turned eagerly in that direction. A stranger stepped boldly in. Handsome, silver-haired, and of an incredible height. He had just made a rapid dizzying ascent from the south, intending to stop but briefly at this inviting watering hole for a beer. As chance would have it, and oddly, he found that he was expected, like a long lost son. He was greeted warmly by a mass of welcoming faces, and confronted by one bewitching heart-shaped one, cool eyes on a level with his. *Well hey,* he said to himself, as they hailed him in to join the party. He cracked a smile and stretched his arms wide, embracing the whole room.

At which point, Janine demanded of Lucille, 'Okay, *where* is he? What have you done with him?'

Lucille smirked.

Georgiana complimented Frank on her brooch, a silverfish that immediately dashed across Frank's shoulder and down into her shirt. 'Oh,' Georgiana said, 'how pretty.' And then, vaguely, 'Do you smell smoke?'

Mike Love passed by carrying a tray of champagne, Mike the

dog tucked under his other arm, earless, but dressed to kill like a rat in a bow tie. Rosie the fortuneteller was reading rum-sodden tea leaves in the corner, sweating in her efforts to keep abreast of the future. 'I see a mysterious stranger,' she predicted, 'a birth, a marriage ... aha! A disaster!'

Mary Stinchcombe, unsteadily balanced on a barstool, tossed her bashed wildflower bouquet, filling the air with pollen and fluff. Reverend Neary, hair sprigged with cleavers, hiccuped loudly.

A clattering *thump* sounded on the stairs.

The gathering hushed. One thought surged like a wave through the room: *Here comes Harold.*

Frank alone guessed otherwise. She would know that sound – a body falling – anywhere. Who else would it be but Hi Henry come to usher her home?

Expecting that Harold might turn up, Lucille had already gone round collecting the bets from those who had lost faith in him. Pockets stuffed, she suddenly thought of Clive, and glancing out the window past the ledge where Tiger was dreaming, racing with icing on his paws through a wind-haunted green field, she saw the Cadillac consumed in flames.

Mary Stinchcombe, about to topple off the stool, about to hurtle into labour, pitched her bouquet again with all the force she could muster, and the tallest man in the bar of the Belvedere Hotel reached out to catch it.

## Bride with Blue Curls

ONCE, I WAS a visitor in a country where leaves are the common currency. A pocketful of silvery-backed poplar could buy you a meal or a clear glass of water. Maple leaves, wide as open hands, catalpa big as platters, would get you more: a shank of land, a twist of river. Real estate that you bought one day, and forgot about the next. The border of this country, where money had veins and turned brown if hoarded, was like a length of skipping rope skimming under your feet: you were in it; you were not.

The citizens of this underpopulated place rarely encountered one another. Though I saw a woman there once I recognized. I'd seen her somewhere before. Down by the lake, on the rocks, in the curling blue waves. She took off her dress, letting it fall like snow among the roots of a laurel, and climbed up. She was sure-footed, a swift and elegant climber. Up she went until she reached the topmost branches which she rode dangerously, arms thrust out. In any other country but this one, I might have feared for her life.

Many women cross borders in high spirits, with great bravado. They never look back.

Like Molly Scott, a friend of my mother's, a war bride from Glasgow. She was a tough one, my mother said, raised with eight brawling brothers. After a whirlwind courtship she married her Canadian soldier and soon found herself touching down on the prairies amid a grim-faced pack of farmers, her new family. One morning, the mother-in-law rolled up her sleeves and declared, *Well, now, we're going to teach you to bake bread.*

*Like hell you are,* was Molly's answer.

'She gave the old bat a push,' my mother reported happily, 'and knocked her over on her arse.'

Molly would not be cowed, nor resented for stealing some mousy farm girl's man. Nor would she eat, let alone make, that manure rising in the pans. She wanted sliced white bread and she got it.

I liked this story because it reminded me of a friend of my own who was born, according to her mother, without anyone's help. She kicked her way out, sprinting down the birth canal and landing in the world feet first. A roustabout from day one, it was felt she'd need the strictures of a feminine name, and her parents tried to corset her with two. They christened her Daphne Diane, but Deedee she came to be called, a name that did not simper or waver demurely, but fired itself directly at you, leaving a pellet-sized hole in your brain.

Deedee was a summer friend, someone I played with three weeks of the year when her parents drove up from Ohio to stay at our tourist camp. Howard, her father, spent his vacation out on the lake fishing, while her mother Dot lay on the beach tanning in salmon-pink shorts and a leopard-skin halter top. Dot was reflectively indolent, though Howard was no philosopher, no mystic. He approached the lake like a businessman, appearing on the dock at seven o'clock sharp every morning, appropriately suited for the job, tackle box in hand in lieu of a brief case. He worked the water for profit, fishing well over the limit, then storing his contraband catch in our deep-freeze. ('Yank,' we said, a word that in under-the-counter camp reference bulged with a prohibited sentiment.) When it was time to pack up and head home, Howard's genius briefly surged to the fore. He artfully concealed fish in the car, behind seats, tucked in gloves, under sun visors (you had to squint the whole way to Ohio, or get a lapful), in Kleenex boxes, in the laundry bag wrapped in Dot's underwear ('No sir, they wouldn't dare touch that!'). Even the leopard-skin halter top that had laboured to hold her warm browning breasts departed stiff with frozen fillets.

Like compatriots, children have no trouble finding each other. A homeland springs up instantly between them, no introductions necessary. My knowing Deedee was never slight and had no beginning as far as I can remember. With her, one was always in the thick of it, holding on tight as she rushed to the very centre of her lunatic existence. That ghost pawing at the window would be her, who else would take my sleep and dreams from me? Who but Deedee would turn them into midnight thievery? It scared me witless sneaking through the cottages at night. We crept into stuffy shuttered bedrooms to steal things from under the snoring noses of the tourists. Our hands slid into pockets searching for cash, into dresser drawers groping for anything interesting, preferably indecent. Once I touched a mouse and her hand flew over my mouth like a choking rag. This was straightforward fun for Deedee, especially if she could get a rise the next day, displaying her booty. Something filched from a little kid, say, that would provoke a tearful, 'That's mine!' And from Deedee, a cool 'Prove it.'

Everything belonged to her and the sooner people got that through their heads the better. She untied boats from the dock. To set them adrift, or more often to treat me to hair-raising rides, taking every possible chance with the unseen, the unanticipated. Sudden shoals, islands rising out of darkness. Did she know what she was doing? I couldn't tell, though she never cracked up the boat or got us lost. When she felt like a swim, she would glide easily alongside a looming flank of rock and climb up, daredevil diving into unfamiliar water smooth as black satin. In storm, lightning stabbed at our backs the way we spiked suckers in the creek with sharp sticks.

My role was that of accomplice, shadow, the unwilling weaker half. I was the conscience who was always expected to say, and who did say, 'Do you really think we should?'

By nature I was cautious, wary of extremes – death and disgrace – and my transformation into the kind of person she wanted was painful, like sewing on a second skin.

(If at night you stand under trees animate in a high wind, as we did, the leaves will roar in your ears like the lake trying to tell you something.)

'What's this?' my mother demanded, holding up a piece of foolscap forgotten in my room. For my edification and amusement, Deedee had illustrated the mechanics of the penis. The first was a sorry character, shrivelled and hangdog, though the second appeared to be waking, harkening to some call. The third was perpendicular. And the last, joyous, elevated to the heights and spurting talking sperm. 'Yahoo!' they whooped, and 'Bingo!' when they hit pay dirt (also illustrated). Had I managed a guileless or puzzled expression, I might have retreated safely into innocence, but the way seemed blocked.

In one particular Deedee was oddly conventional. At night we roved and pulled pranks. But during the long afternoons we played wedding. Hers was to be an opulent affair which we planned and enacted inch by tedious inch. We began at the rehearsal party – to which she was inviting most of her grade five class – and slogged on through to the honeymoon in Hawaii. I had by heart the details of the dress, how it would be made of old French lace and silk and embroidered seed pearls, with a train as long as a comet's icy tail. She would float down the aisle on Howard's arm, wear the same diamond tiara Dot had worn at her wedding, carry a bouquet of roses, orchids, baby's breath, and blue curls. She promised (or threatened) to throw this bouquet directly at me in the lineup of grasping single women, because naturally I would be desperate if I kept growing at the present rate, my options limited to basketball players and giants.

'What about the bodice?' Deedee asked. 'The neckline, curved, low-cut? I'd look terrific in that.'

'But you don't have, you know, breasts.'

'They're on order. What do you think, moron?'

I was to be the maid of honour. In the meantime, while she paraded the beach dressed in old sheers and carrying wildflowers, I filled in for the groom. That poor faceless sap, a living tuxedo basically. His person was the one detail in the whole fabulous design that seemed to be of least significance.

In truth, my experience of weddings was limited and had gotten entangled with my experience of funerals. This may have had something to do with my grandfather, who was in the habit of marrying women who died off shortly afterward – a liability when you're dating among the euchre and shuffleboard set. Also, the school I went to didn't make much distinction between the two, or at least that's the impression I got. It was a small Catholic school, close to the church, and if there was a high mass being celebrated, the students were often sent over. Perhaps this was seen as some kind of educational field trip, like our annual day off to attend the cattle sale, or we may simply have been filling in as extras. For whatever reason, we'd be herded together and marched across the schoolyard like a pint-sized column of hired weepers or celebrants. We filed into the back pews, whispery, fidgety, and above all curious – what was it to be this time, marriage or death? But since the adults up front got the best seats and blocked our view, and because the incense and heat and Latin quickly induced a kind of torpor, we seldom saw more than a white hem whisking by, or the edge of a creaking coffin being wheeled up the aisle.

We were segregated, boys on one side of the church, girls on the other. I suppose the boys were kept busy enough. The usual monkey business, punching and elbowing each other on the sly, while we girls exchanged covert looks or secretly passed around some token – a note, a ring. The thing was, we couldn't waggle or nod our heads too vigorously in case the stiff rectangles of toilet paper we were obliged to wear as head covering slid off. If you were someone like Christine Jolly, a 'flying squirrel' in the reading hierarchy of the classroom, you would have the foresight to carry a kerchief or a plastic rain hat in your pocket. Exposing those tiny white teeth, an orthodontic elastic band around the two front ones – her future smile assured – Christine would produce just such an object with a neat flourish before everyone's envious eyes. But if you were like the rest of us, unaspiring rodents when it came to reading, foragers, gnawing on the unpronounceable, then you'd have to struggle with bobby pins trying to attach paper slippery and wayward as the Holy Ghost to the top of your head. But of course it was not the Holy Ghost – it was 'bumwad', as the boys called it, doing symbolic work for a change. The stuff was light in substance, but it bore down with a certain weight: Our hair was shameful. We'd been told that in

Biblical times women's hair was beautiful, so alluring that it distracted men's attention away from the Lord and had to be covered. I expect that our tangled, frizzy, and unwashed hair was only shameful to our mothers, who raked combs through it and tugged savagely until tears spurted from our eyes. I thought of the Queen's green hair on the one-dollar bill I had been shown, how if you folded it a certain way, her curls depicted the devil's face. If I grew my hair long and got a perm, I wondered, would he come nest in mine?

Both Deedee and Dot had American hair. It was restless, worn up and down in so many different styles it seemed to speak. Nothing could have possessed it that wouldn't have been instantly rinsed out with vinegar or beer, or peroxided, pincurled, screwed up into a tight twist, clipped into a new moon bob, or flung over a shoulder. Dot's hair even had a scandalous past, this involving her first husband. ('First!' I exclaimed to Deedee. This was information I didn't know what to do with – in our country you only got one.) The man was sensible in most respects, she said, except that he was obsessed with her hair. 'They like it long, honey,' Dot explained, a plait of smoke curling out the side of her mouth, 'makes it easier to drag you outa the cave.' She said he played with her hair like it was a toy, like it was gold, sifting and stroking it, fondling it until her head ached. He measured it once a week with a ruler from his protractor set. He couldn't sleep at night unless his hands were buried in it and there were times he woke in the morning with strands of it wound tightly around blue fingers. He refused to let her have it cut, and when she finally convinced him that it wouldn't grow unless it was trimmed up a bit, he insisted she bring home the trimmings in a bag which he saved.

'Split ends? Girls, I looked like a human fork.'

On hair cutting days he followed her to the beauty parlour. He dodged behind buildings and cars, then hung around outside, peeking in whenever he got the chance.

'Honestly, I was sick to death of it, so one day I said to

Leeann, my hairdresser, let's get rid of this stuff, and she said *are you sure,* and I said, cut it off, Leeann.'

By the time her husband figured out what was happening and flew in, it was too late, her hair was already sliding to the floor. She said he kind of groaned and sank to his knees and touched it like it was a dead cat. He scooped it up and buried his face in it and some stuck to his cheeks, wet from crying, 'poor bugger'. Or 'booger', as Dot pronounced it.

'I'm telling you, that's when he went right off his nut. He whipped out his handgun and started shooting, BAM BAM like that, and then there was hairspray exploding and Dippity-do hitting the walls, and the row of ladies sitting under the hair dryers looked up from their movie magazines *real* annoyed, and I left.

'Now you take Howard,' she spat a shred of tobacco from the tip of her tongue, aiming it toward the lake, 'he wouldn't care bugfuck (oops, sorry, dear) if I was bald. He's a leg man.'

This was no surprise. Dot's calves were like long white pike bellies basking that first day on the beach, glistening with a mixture of baby oil and iodine, about to be fried. Deedee and I took to our heels. We ran and ran and didn't stop, except to get married or to eat. She made French toast and beanie weenies – to me, foreign cuisine – and turned the air violet with her foul tongue if grease snapped out of the pan to dance on her arm.

To witness your child being invaded and overtaken by another is rough on a parent. 'You sound American,' was my mother's criticism, alarmed to hear me spout Deedee's notions and enthusiasms and in *her* accent. Like a lackey, a disciple, my knowable self so readily ditched. Deedee liked what she saw, she liked what I reflected of her. She could put her hand on me and leave a mark, though not indelible.

One time we were playing with some other kids on the dock, and on impulse – nothing Deedee urged, her presence alone an incitement – I pushed a boy off the end into deep water. I knew he couldn't swim and he almost drowned. The two of us tore up the hill to hide, frightened, excited, and Deedee praised me. She said it served him right, he was asking for it (he asked for nothing). Then added, 'Too bad I won't be seeing you any more, they'll send you to reformatory school now.'

What I should say is that when I did go, not to reformatory school, but to that country where money grows on trees, where you can use it to purchase the sky, I went alone. If Deedee saw me there swaying in the crown of an ailanthus, tree-of-heaven, stuffing my pockets with a free hand, my head hallowed with light, she couldn't get to me. She had no passport, and no invitation.

Ohio is the buckeye state. The 'fetid buckeye' it is sometimes called, leaves elliptical, palmately compound, poisonous when young. The bark of the buckeye is also toxic, though was once used medicinally, as its seeds were carried in pioneers' pockets to ward off rheumatism. Faith in trees. In the past a dying child would have been passed through the branches of an ash to find in its generous green breadth a cure. The redbud and the linden have heart-shaped leaves. The rowan is said to have escaped north along ditches. Though if you were to fall into a swiftly flowing river, thick with current, under willows with sweeping fronds, they would not save you. Leaves spent on the water are just leaves carried downstream.

My friendship with Deedee ended where it had begun, somewhere in the middle. It was Howard's fault, really. He eventually caught the 'big one', but he must have caught it in his teeth, because he went over the side of the boat and never came back up. There didn't seem to be much weeping and wailing – it was all kept fairly hush-hush, dead customers being bad for business. Deedee never returned to the camp after that, although Dot did come back one more time. A few years later she showed up with her new husband. ('Can you *beat* that?' my mother said.) But they only stayed a week as the weather was bad.

I began to notice then a peculiar thing. Adults are loath to let go of each other. Even people they don't particularly like. My mother hugged Dot and promised to keep in touch, which was a ludicrous promise, they both knew. She stood waving as their car passed through the front gate and under the sign upon which my father had stencilled with black paint the message: 'Will ye no come back again.' The ambiguity of this parting Scotticism seemed to please the tourists to no end, and might have been the hook that did bring them back to us year after year.

But this loose kind of fidelity, made of words and not much else, was not an issue with us. Deedee and I hadn't even bothered to say goodbye. Nor did I even think of her after that, except to wonder if her dream-wedding came off, if Mr. X finally developed features and materialized in his tux at the right moment.

People go under. And I guess what happens, getting older, you grow these arms like branches for them to grab onto before they slip beyond memory, crossing over into a country where you cannot follow.

That woman who climbed the tree, I thought her head was flying apart, but what I was seeing was a scattering mass of Adonis blue, a rare species of butterfly, that had settled in her hair.

# A Bird Story

*for Don McKay and Nancy McLeod*

*You weren't born, you were hatched,* Henry's father used to say. Henry's brother Arnie they found behind the couch, a ball of dust and dog hair and thread loosely hanging together the way Arnie does when he shuffles into town on a Saturday night. Muriel came in a basket of apples, a fresh red-cheeked child with a swirl of golden delicious hair. Phyllis scooped her up out of the basket and shouted down to Dayland who was making whirligigs in the basement, *It's a girl!* Arnie, too, had been a surprise. *My goodness,* Phyllis said as she slid the couch aside during spring cleaning and Arnie rolled out, *a big one.* But Henry was another story – a long difficult birth. He sat on the kitchen counter for two years in a homemade eggcup, one of Dayland's old bowling trophies, picking up coffee stains and specks of grease from the fry pan. He annoyed Phyllis. He cluttered up the counter, he got in her way. He was *useless.* Eventually she quilted a cover for Henry and stuck him between the toaster and blender. There he hummed quietly to himself and, in a manner of speaking, cooked.

Then one night, the moon a bulging eye weeping silver on bats' wings, a night so clear you could hear snakes singing arias on the rocks, Henry, egged on perhaps by this witchery in the air, finally cracked. *I'll be damned,* said Phyllis as she flapped into the kitchen the next morning and saw him wriggling helplessly on the counter. She washed him in the sink, diapered him in a gingham tea towel, then placed him on the porch nestled in an eyrie of blankets. He jerked and waved his little starfish hands at the two curious faces bobbing in front of him. Arnie's slapdash features – lopsided smile, boxer's nose, odd-coloured eyes, red springing Dagwood hair – cadged a first delighted chortle from baby Henry, and Muriel's face, round as a dish and rosy, dimpled with mischief, unwhorled his heart like a fern. *This is great,* he thought, settling in, lulled by the comforting sound of his mother breaking dishes and smashing pots in the kitchen, when suddenly Dayland emerged from the basement. A monster with hair on his face and a full black shadow trailing like a garbage bag behind him. He loomed and leered, wanting to get a good look at his son, and Henry couldn't help himself. He screamed. A wild shriek, a thin shrill wire of sound that pierced and strung their ears together. Honey the cat, a sunny blaze of fur, hit the screen, shredding a whole generation of fleas. Dust and dander began to boil off Arnie like a beaten rug. Henry screamed again and his cry, amplified, skipped around the perimeter of the bay, hemming it like a huge skirt. Dogfish whimpered like spaniels. Hawks picked up the fear in it and carried it for miles.

Dayland trudged back downstairs. He snapped on the light and it buzzed like an angry bee. *Why,* he addressed his whirligigs, Wily Coyote, Sylvester, Elmer Fudd, *why can't we have normal kids? Why,* he asked the furnace, *why can't they be like the Priddles'? Every one of them straight out of Vergie's potato patch. Nice kids. Yeah, okay, a little thick, but nice.* He grabbed a hammer and scratched his head with the claw, thoroughly perplexed.

Like any mother worth her salt, Phyllis blamed herself. If every dead moth and fungus spore gravitated to Arnie and encircled him like a planetary ring, it was her fault for not vacuuming high enough. If Muriel had tiny leaf-shaped ears that listened too intently, that was because a drop of Irish blood, green as chlorophyll, had worked its elfin trickery through Phyllis's side of the family. As for Henry, well, that was as plain as the tuberous nose on Elsie Priddle's face. Phyllis's childhood nickname was to blame. *Bird Legs* her brothers called her when she was a tiny chattering thing with sticks for limbs. *Bird Legs* they taunted, and it stuck. Other names applied in malice or in fun, flicked idly at her like beer foam, simply melted away. Bird Legs alone twirled in the dust and flew through childhood, emerging in high school transformed. No longer a skinny sparrow-faced girl but a larger blossoming creature, warm and full-bodied as a cinnamon teal. *A looker,* said Peal Lewis. *A real dish,* according to Harless Lozier. Both grade nine boys at the time making their own transitions from BB guns and gobbing off the town dock to dances at the Shaftsbury Hall and puking a purée of lemon gin and hot dog down the back steps. At these dances it was apparent that Phyllis's nickname had grown up with her; it rolled off people's tongues like praise. It buoyed her up as she swept around the hall, feet flying, heart pounding, chrysanthemum curls bouncing. She rarely sat down to catch her breath, the boys wouldn't let her. It was not for Bird Legs to know the anguish of wallflowers, girls like Maisie Blue or the Wood sisters, who sank deep coiling roots into the sidelines and soured there like old milk.

Phyllis met Dayland at the Shaftsbury. He was from the west end of the island and looked it. He was darker, denser, greasier than the boys from the east, who carried a certain light in their eyes and on their skin. Dayland was a bear out of a cave and just as grumpy. His fists sprang into the air and hovered like birds of prey at the slightest provocation. Like hapless Buddy Worth stabbing him in the ankle with his new pointy-toed shoe and almost getting his block knocked off. Phyllis intervened and Dayland was hers. He tagged after her the rest of the evening, persistently cutting in on her other partners. She disliked him. But that summer night handfuls of stars had been tossed like confetti into the sky and a slow kind of magic rose off the lake and drifted into the hall where it moved lazily among the dancers, relaxing their clenched hearts and lavishing them with gifts. Fred McClay, two hundred pounds teetering on two left feet, suddenly couldn't be touched for agility and grace. Flashes of beauty redefined homely inbred faces and currents churned in minds that had long been pools of floating duckweed. As for Dayland, something about him diffuse and wayward came together, like darkness condensing into mystery, that gave him an edge, a strange unprecedented attraction. Put off by his gruffness, his fat grasping fingers and barnyard smell (*pigshit,* her heightened sensitivities told her), Phyllis nevertheless found herself drawn to him as a mouse to the ghostly heart-shaped face of a barn owl. As she left with him that night – he took her home by way of twisting dirt roads and a field with rushing waves of grass and blue pools of chicory that whispered against them – someone called her name. A disembodied and sorrowful voice followed her down the steps and into the dark cab of Dayland's truck. And it followed her still. Doing the wash or the ironing she'd hear a faint *Bird Legs, Bird Legs,* like a waif calling. A small disquieting voice that sang its disappointment and mourned her loss. That cooed and scolded, pulling her back in time, leaving her staring into space. That wove an ever tightening cage around her life.

So Phyllis often stood watching her youngest swooping around the yard or singlemindedly digging for worms in the garden, and a portion of guilt, about the size of an ostrich egg, would roll off the roof and land on her head. Or sneak up from behind like a gigolo and goose her. Because with Henry it was never airplanes, but swifts; never cowboys and Indians, but sharks and shearwaters. When most toddlers were babbling *birdie birdie* at any creature with wings, Henry would say of a speck miles away on the rocks, *look, black-crowned night heron.* He knew chickens the way most boys know hockey players. *Andalusian, black Spanish, blue Orpington, Jersey white giant, speckled Sussex.* He recited long lists happily to Arnie who accepted any kind of information, no matter how peculiar, from anyone. To Muriel, swaying in the treetops, he told secrets about local birdlife, matters of sex and family, shamelessly disclosing even the tiny skeletons in their closets. She envisioned a vast and resonant soap opera taking place all around them with episodes begun in the bushes concluding romantically in the clouds, or along the lake in huge drifting kettles.

Dayland, on the other hand, viewed ornithology as an overlong and obscene word. *Alls you got to know about birds,* he would say, *is some are yellow, some are brown.* Muttering to himself over breakfast, he threatened to take Henry into town to see a doctor.

Phyllis stood firm in the doorway, a block of stone, saying that if he took Henry he'd surely have to take the others. Wasn't Arnie just as bad with his hoard of empty spaghetti tins and shampoo bottles, or Muriel, who was no end of trouble, practically living outside. Not that Phyllis wasn't worried about Henry. Oh no, worry was a piece of work never finished. He was enough to drive a brood of mothers to distraction. When he wasn't jumping head first nighthawk-style off the shed, he was practising mating displays in front of her bridge club, or risking his life at the supper table by parroting everything Dayland happened to say. His moods were as erratic as the flight patterns of swallows. He suffered migratory restlessness in the fall. A week of frenzied activity, stockpiling food and packing his knapsack, was followed by a sudden swing into depression. As the flocks gathered and left one by one for the Bahamas and Mexico, a sickness seized him. He spent days sitting by the picture window in the living room, staring out, the sky unyielding as a test pattern. His only consolation was Honey, a mass of gold curled in his lap, purring out her own nostalgic longing for the savoury taste of meadowlark, the succulence of dove.

Then duck season opened. Night after night Henry dreamed he was falling. Dreamed of pain shooting through him like an electric wire as he plummeted into black water. His father the shadowy figure that splashed toward him, gun in hand.

As always it was a relief to see a skin of ice forming on the lake and the first flakes of snow jiving like midges above it. Winter would enter with a slap and set Henry to rights. His forlorn face took on a pale saintly expression. Meagre rations kept him alive; the friendly buzz of a chickadee, starlings squabbling over a crust, the disappearing wingtip of a snowy owl, white as an apparition. His passion went underground and germinated there like the sprouting plants and grasses that were tickling the great duck-soft underbelly of snow that covered everything. He descended into the basement and worked beside his father *like a real boy*. Together they made Tweety Birds and Woody Woodpeckers to give away for Christmas, while the furnace ate enormous helpings of coal and pitched heat around the room like an old demon.

As long as winter ruled, butting up against the house and freezing the plumbing, the family huddled close, tightly packed as a pod. Oddly, under these conditions, they fitted more easily together. While the cold drove hungry wolves around the lake and mixed bitter concoctions of ice and wind, they felt safe, nestled in self-generated warmth. But at the first microscopic hint of spring in the air, solidarity began to thaw.

Ambling into the kitchen one morning frowzy as a hound dog's rug, Arnie would catch an evil look from his mother, or get a slap on the head from Dayland, who would claim to have seen a pair of flies screwing behind his ear. Muriel might start flipping soggy cereal at him, or Honey arch her back and hiss. Would this upset Arnie? Not in the least. This was a sign. The season, however imperceptibly, had changed. Almost within reach, below thinning layers of snow, lay a bounty of last year's refuse, discoloured, swollen as the drowned, though to Arnie's eye as lovely and artfully arranged as any spring floral display.

Henry, tuned in to a collective idea swelling in the south like an enormous sun bulging below the horizon, was already pacing the floor. He'd been on the alert from the moment the first whistling swan, gliding majestically across a lake near Lumpkin, Georgia, raised its long neck, pointed its slender black beak north, and thought *hmmm*. By the time the sky was filled with the ocean roar of beating wings, excitement drove him into a frenetic, twittering state. He was unable to sit or eat, or even speak without tearing his words into syllabic shreds. And then there was the other problem. This was the time of year when boys from town rode out on their bikes, later in cars, to court Muriel – they'd swing like monkeys from tree to tree trying to catch up with her. Arnie was gone for days, returning home even scruffier, with weeds in his hair and shirt buttons swinging loose on single threads. An outbreak of spring fever meant they had to put up with the nuisance and embarrassment of Henry's infatuations. One year a pretty little warbler might catch his eye, the next an indigo bunting or a Baltimore oriole. He fell for flashy tanagers and yellow dancers, flittering redstarts and duplicitous catbirds. Once he was smitten by a common weatherworn gull and spent the summer madly filleting fish while it stood on the dock and screeched at him like a querulous wife. Some of these heart throbs lived on in family memory: the dissolute Bohemian waxwing that devoured fermented berries then flew in crazy drunken circles trilling loudly until it smacked into the side of the house; the unrequited turkey vulture that hovered and hovered and would not go away; the much lamented European goldfinch that Honey ate, colourful fieldmarks bleeding like paint out of her mouth. Certain special ones Henry alone cherished, like the timorous loon that called to him every evening over the moon-streaked bay, the flirtatious tail-wagging phoebe, the thrush that wanted his hair for her nest, his lips for her fledglings, and the hummingbird, a Cuban emerald, that materialized like a quivering jewel before his eyes then vanished forever.

An endlessly unfurling list, a lifetime of fowl fancies and flames might have been Henry's lot if it hadn't been for Raphael. Admittedly, neither fanfare nor flashing lights marked his arrival on the scene, but for the family, soon to be unwittingly herded into their renaissance, it was a significant event.

Henry discovered him on the shore one morning, lying limp on a rock. *Hurt*, he immediately concluded, whereas Raphael was simply indulging in one of his favourite activities: sleep. When Henry burst into the kitchen carrying his newfound treasure (what to Phyllis looked like a huge pair of argyle socks rolled up into a ball), Dayland had a fit. Cigarette smoke pouring out of his nostrils, beads of dribbled coffee rolling down his chin, he shouted, *Jesus-another-goddamn-dead-bird-get-that-thing-out-of-here!* At which point Raphael cocked open a dark defiant eye and stared straight at him. He leafed quickly through Dayland's mind as if it were a grade one primer. Then he surveyed the whole sorry lot, shaking his head sadly as one would at the victims of some unspeakable disaster. Slopping up cereal, sucking on toast, snarling at one another, they stirred in him a sense of mission. They *needed* him. It was obvious. They needed him as an infant needs a mother, as a body needs a soul. This must have been the moment that *the wild kingdom* (as Raphael was to hear it described on TV) planted one large webbed foot immovably in the door.

Raphael's own mother wasn't surprised when she heard that her son had wormed his way into a human household and into human hearts, small as they are. He'd always been the odd one out, a snot from the word go. Even as an egg he tried to roll himself away from the others in the nest. He had the vanity of a peacock, the cunning of a crow, and he was lazy like his father, forever squawking to ride on her back while Gavriel, Euphemia, Ora and Umbriel paddled behind. He used to pester her with questions about them. *What do they do in those houses? Do they have any kind of spiritual life, any capacity for thought?* She hadn't been the one to encourage him. She told him the truth. That they're sick. The species has an incurable illness which makes them unpredictable. One minute they're studying you, worshipping you, painting eggs and wearing feathers, and the next they're wringing your neck and stirring up gravy to pour over your carcass. Might as well go and live with ogres as far as Raphael's mother was concerned. *She* would never sink so low.

At first the family didn't think much of it. They tolerated him. He was quiet, and *kinda cute*, though always underfoot. In the basement he was an attentive audience to Dayland's soliloquies, and in the kitchen he watched as Phyllis sobbed into the cake batter (tears being the secret ingredient that gave her baking that special tangy flavour). He listened closely to confidences from Muriel and Arnie, but especially from Henry who seemed to interest him the most. Empathetic, loyal as a winged Lassie, he ascended through the ranks. Companion, analyst, mentor ... double agent.

He infiltrated the family's dreams and worked there with a viral intensity. He dived below the surface of their lives and rode the undercurrent, ducked below the swampy miasma of emotion and probed where sensitive roots were knotted into a ball. He undermined their sadness, strong in humans as musk, and diffused the anger that made them blow apart then come together again like hands squeezing and kneading. He introduced the comic element. Humour travelled around the supper table like salmonella. They began to find one another mildly entertaining, then ridiculously funny. Indeed, a bright and whimsical mood took hold, as though a narcotic spice had been slipped into the familial stew.

Phyllis lightened up and nibbled with more amusement at her life. She lost weight and dyed her hair. She stopped hearing those voices, or at least if the Jello salad addressed her its message was not unpleasant. The nattering past slid off her back like an incubus tired of the game. She bustled blithe and unburdened into home renovation: knocking down walls, stripping wood, hanging plants, painting ceilings blue as a budgie's nostril. She threw open the windows and light splashed in like bleach. It chewed up the shadows and spat them out as lace – Dayland's like a bride's frothy train swishing behind him as he wandered outside to gaze at the sky. This a newfound pastime. For heaven no longer gaped back at him the way it used to, but had taken him under its wide arching wing. Sent him blessings in warm caressing breezes and showers of inspiration. Ideas jammed into his mind like a multitude of stations vying for one channel on the radio. He hummed, he whistled. Then, picking up a distress signal, he'd rush back inside to open another can of peas for the cat, who lately had become a vegetarian.

Nor were the others immune to this new ambience. The shards and fragments of Arnie's creative genius finally cohered. The mass of odds and ends he'd been collecting all his life began surging like an enormous river into place. He built a car out of broken hockey sticks; a patio out of Dixie cups and those flat wooden spoons. Anything missing, he supplied; anything broken, he fixed. He was invaluable, ever ready with ancient furry bottles of glue and used bits of Scotch tape to mend and hold in place a disintegrating material world.

Parental pride swelled. Muriel, as well, pleased her mother by dropping out of the trees one night like a ripened spy and landing in the arms of Curtis Mead, a budding naturalist out studying the effect of moonlight on the reproductive cycle of the firefly. The family welcomed him wholeheartedly into their midst. *She might have brought home a squirrel,* Dayland pointed out philosophically.

As for Henry, why he became his mother's favourite, her darling, her pet. She now greeted friends in the grocery store by digging in her purse for show-off photos: one of Henry rowing on the lake with Raphael perched like a figurehead on the bow; one of him clowning, fanning Raphael like a sultan and feeding him chocolates; and a more recent picture of him on a beach in Florida where he drove Raphael every winter.

Miraculously, Henry's nature had settled; his obsession came to roost, tucking and folding itself almost invisibly away. It took a rare bird these days to move him over to the window from his comfortable perch in front of the TV. Dayland, gesturing expansively, laying before his son wonders freshly gleaned from the sky, could scarcely stir an ember of interest. Henry was like a monk or a holy man whose meditative investments had finally paid off in cool tranquillity. Contentment surrounded him on all sides, enclosing him completely.

Given an aerial view, a bird's-eye view if you will, you could even say he looked happier than most, like a child reading a story, absorbed, and totally at ease with whatever anthropomorphic detail might crop up.

# A Laughing Woman

A LAUGHING WOMAN with flame-coloured hair and a dress
green as leaves wanders down the road and it's summer, luminous summer, the sun dropping haloes and scarves of light.
Clothes are cast off, shades are raised. Putty-soft babies, born
and coddled in the long winter, are put out on lush new grass and
later, in photos, are seen to be playing with sunspots and flashing
bolts. Summer spreads over the island like a thousand voices
carried over water, like a thousand tongues of fire, engulfing,
inciting.

Even the ghosts, packed like larvae in the earth, grow restless
and refuse to stay put. Mari knows this. Within sight of her
place, down the hill on the other side of the road, lies a graveyard. Evenings sitting on the front step with Whip beside her,
chasing birds in his sleep, she watches them rise like brume.
Some drift toward town, others stay close, anchored to the last of
their possessions – mossy bones, names carved on stone, a spelling of themselves they no longer understand. It fascinates her,
how they weave like swifts through the falling dark caught in patterns of unrest that never vary. Walking endless circles, replaying
snagged shreds of their lives, re-enacting their deaths. One
searches in the grass for spiders, another, thin and flickering,
waits by the edge of the bush for the woman who shot him during
deer season. Orie Lewis, who lost his life in the sawmill, hovers
by his grave, phantom muscles piled on his back like cumulus
clouds. The three wives of Dunk Purcell, all named Doris and
all a lambent blue, link arms and float off together, leaving Dunk
to rot.

If only her lost boy were as concentrated as a ghost, Mari can't
help thinking. God knows, he's everywhere, like the sound of the
water. He's the shadow beneath the boat, arms flecked with red
paint, his hair swirls around him. He speaks to cats, luring them
in on a silky smooth line. Wild roses and tiger lilies at his funeral.

But no body. *He budded on earth,* whispered Sister St. Anne, *to bloom in heaven.* Well, he *was* just a boy, eighteen, nineteen, not much older. Claimed he came from a place on the other side of the island where they name their children after rivers. One day she noticed him down in the graveyard leaning against a wooden marker. A bunch of kids from town were playing tag, zig-zagging and whirling around him. They dodged behind gravestones, knocked over wreaths, leapt screaming over fresh mounds. She guessed that he had taken up with them like a stray, as drifters do. Sucked into the centre of a game that flowed like light from hand to flying ankle. Or, perhaps they followed him. Wolf-dark, subterranean, damp sweet smell. Her drowned boy, bending down to kiss the water. Water leaching the colour out of his hair, translucent now, undulating with the weeds, a nest for fish eggs.

Uncle Ryder left a black bass on her doorstep, the Misses Tinkus from across the bay a basket of cherry tomatoes. From town, a litany of looks. From Father Boddy, a boozy caress. Handfuls of grass Mari tore out of the ground, green whistling ribbons of grass, the crush of clover and nettles and rue. *Where,* she asks the cat and the fallen-down fence, *is he?* Where in all the waters of the world? Will his bones return in the rain someday tapping on the pane? Every year spring unlocks the ice and he drifts further away, only the tide of memory to pull him back. If she could open his eyes, touch lips and hands, count the scars, birthmarks, watermark.

Mari didn't know whether to believe in him or not. That first day he walked up the road with heat and dust swirling around him, Whip went crazy barking, hurling himself against the fence. And him chewing a stem of grass, taking his sweet time, driving the dog wild. He spoke quietly. Said he was looking for work, that he didn't want much in return, room and board would do. She needed a handyman, why not, he could sleep in the boat-house. She found a brush and a can of red paint, then pointed out the path that led to the cottages. Whip curled himself into a rigid ball, growling deep thundery curses.

She gave him plenty of chances to get away, to run off with her money, her life, whatever it was he wanted. She sent him to town in the truck and he always returned with food, bait, beer and a wad of cash stuffed in his back pocket. Roaring past Mrs. Leander Hall's place, the old woman rocking on the porch would think, how nice to have a boy like him on hand, with those tight black pants and that purring voice. Very nice, indeed.

He told Mari that he'd once had a jacket that was fringed with gulls' bones and dried ducks' feet which clattered like castanets when he danced. He told her how to strip a tree, how to make baskets out of black ash. He told her he could stay underwater longer than anyone else alive.

Mari wakes from dreams full of storm and people shouting, someone lying on the ground covered with wet leaves. Someone, herself, buried in stones. Flat clattering stones that, as she rises, tumble into bright patterns on the floor. Thirty years ago waking in this same room she saw a woman standing by the window, lacy curtains billowing around her like sails. This was the woman with strong hands who laughing lifted Mari up to the sun. She remembers the wildness in her mother's arms. Being held close to a heart that beat too fast. She sees her in the distance, dazzling as a sunburst, picking birds out of the air, holding their tiny legs like the stems of flowers.

Who is the weeping man in the kitchen? Her father. Her father who lies below across the road, too tired to get up.

Summer mornings Mari tunnels under the covers. She stays in bed until the sun is high and the house begins to pulse with heat. No need to get up early. She closed the camp years ago and no longer has to pump out the boats first thing or mollify the tourists. Hearty lumbering people they were, more demanding than children. She spoiled them with homebaked bread and clean white sheets snapping on the line. She tolerated their jokes and parties and messes; posed for pictures wearing funny hats and holding long stringers of fish. She endured their easily-roused affection. They brought her bottles of Old Crow which they opened themselves and drank the moment they stepped out of their enormous finned cars and settled on her front step.

They loved to talk. Weren't happy unless they were broadcasting to town, revealing family secrets, spending them in the air like small change. When they argued, they clenched their fists and howled abuse. Then lapsed quickly back into humour, hands opening wide as sunflowers.

Though relieved to get rid of them for a while, Mari hated sending them out on the lake, slickered and smiling, expectant. Sometimes he went with them as a guide. If he took them to spots where the fish were biting, their excitement made them dangerous. They jumped around in the lurching boat, casting lines blindly, drawing in more water than fish. They called him *Chief* and slapped him on the back. They pressed silver dollars into his palm which he skipped across the lake when they weren't looking. On the way home – throttle wide open – they scraped over shoals and crashed hooting through whitecaps. Sailed into the bay like heroes. They didn't know enough to drown.

He never came to her room. While snoring tourists fought in their cabins for covers, they met outside by the boathouse. They walked the shoreline a distance before disappearing into the birches, white in the moonlight. Or they wandered up the hill and stretched like shadows in the long grass. On humid nights, the closeness of the day still clinging to them like an extra skin, they dove into the bay. Water absolved them. They swam and forgot about each other and were startled when they touched, arms weaving like snakes.

The easy death some call it. Mari wonders if that could possibly be true. Could changing elements be the same as changing your mind. Slipping without a struggle from one language into another – a lapping laving tongue. What we know here too well, Mari thinks. We're born to the sound, tethered to it like beasts that can't break loose. Ears shaped to gather it, mouths and lungs. Every summer the lake takes its tithe. Sweet-talks one or two; abducts the rest.

No one was concerned the day he went out to search for tourists caught by a sudden storm. Least of all Mari. She thought him incapable of accident. He moved with such certainty, his body profoundly clever. Somehow he made impending danger seem impossible. The storm intensified. Mari knew he would take refuge somewhere when he had to. The missing fishermen straggled back to camp on their own. They crawled onto the dock out of rolling boats, stunned and sick, aware for the first time of what they were dealing with. Their wives, red-eyed and ugly with premature grief, barrelled down the path, rain whipping their legs. They clutched their men like huge helpless infants and shouted prayers of relief that the wind ripped into senseless shreds.

Neighbours, as well as people from town, drove out to Mari's place the next day to wait for the body. Women rose early that morning and arrived with cooked hams, bowls of potato salad, and lemon pies crowned with meringues whipped into wild peaks. They collected on the beach and discussed other drownings, other bodies, where found and in what condition. Children listened intently, savouring the details, which would surface later in their own conversations, gruesomely distorted. Men who had not yet joined in the search jumped into the remaining boats and sped out of the bay, trains of foam frothing behind them. Crazy Larry tapped directly into an illicit undercurrent of delight and milled through the crowd beaming. Father Boddy pulled a silver flask out of the frayed pocket of his black jacket and offered it to Mari. Whip ate a bag of marshmallows and threw up in someone's purse.

By evening the men began drifting back, faces tight and pale with dismay. They found nothing. Not the overturned boat, no clothing, not a trace. He had eluded them. Disappointment in the turning backs of the dispersing party was almost palpable. The police boat was the last to return. It splashed softly like an apparition into the bay. Corporal Green assured Mari that he would turn up somewhere soon, not to worry. She had no intention of worrying. He was gone, his tracks dissolved in dark water.

It's the unquiet deaths that unlace minds. Mari remembers her father running distracted into the field as though her mother had returned in all the yellow dancing flowers. Now she was doing it too, watching, waiting for his return.

His arrival was imminent and would manifest itself in unexpected ways. In the plunging dive of a preying hawk. In the hand that grabs her ankle and pulls her under when she dreams she is swimming. It gets to everyone. People speak to her after church. Tell her they've seen him, alive, working in a lodge twenty miles away. Someone else, down looking for wrecks near Picnic Island, saw him tangled in a billowing cage of weeds. The next time down, though, he was gone. Of course. He's never there when you want him. He's slippery and slight. Stealthy. He used to sneak up from behind, put his arms around her and kiss the nape of her neck. His hands and lips were cold, even then. It made her shudder.

She remembers going into the boathouse once, pressing the door shut against the glowing afternoon, and hearing his voice drifting through the warm musty darkness. She asked him what he was doing there in the middle of the day, and he said, *I'm dead, can't you understand that?*

MARI SITS on the front step watching the sun travel across the yard and up into the trees, setting them on fire before it sinks into the lake. Soon Whip will run up the road with something soft, a mourning dove or a lark, cradled in his mouth. He'll drop it at her feet. Mari will look down and it will be fall. Flaming leaves will tumble out of the trees like a thousand little doors closing on the summer. The ghosts in the graveyard will forget how to get up, and why. In town, blinds will be drawn and babies with blossoming moonfaces will be snatched up and wrapped in blankets before the first cold raindrops shatter on their heads.

# Cutting the Devil's Throat

THAT'S THE Old Viper in the kitchen dropping a half-eaten pear into the stew. Leftover beer, bloated butts aswill in the bottom. An earthblind spud. A moose haunch, hacked up. A green rabbit's foot. A handful of washers. Nails. An onion. A grocery receipt: *$1.98, $3.29*, etc. *Thank you. Have a nice day.* The Old Viper stirs 'er up, ladles 'er out.

That's Geordie, the kid with snot-clotted red hair, freckles like flicked mud on his face, coppers in his belly, rocks in his pocket. On his bike, a metallic blue CCM (borrowed), swim suit looped over the handlebars, he races a black car down the hill, exhaust streaming up his nostrils. One thought flaps like a red ribbon in his head, whip-snapping like a lizard's tongue: *Geordie, you gonna win!*

Over there now, that's Pinkie. Got her round peachbottom planted on a meteorite. Only one in town and her butt's on it. Popped out of the sky one day like a boil. Shouldn't let her appearance fool you. She may look simple, addled, poached, but Pinkie knows the score. And nowhere does it say Geordie wins.

That black Chev chewing up the road, dust purling out of its backend, dark snail of a man curled around the wheel, that's bat-eared Baxter Putt. Owns the general store, runs the post office. Nice guy. Friendly. A worrier though. Brow lowering as he listens to that *rattly-clunk* noise the car makes. He peers into the rearview mirror and gets a fright. Face in there screwed up tight as a gargoyle, horns and fangs (not really). Bax squinches his eyes, looks again. *Ah heck*, he says, foot punching the gas, *that's Geordie.*

And on the dock, that's Thunderhead with the rest of the gang – Doggo, Stretch, and the Meatgrinder – pitching stones into the lake. Grimy boy pawfuls of sandstone and shale, crystal-rich hornfels, egg-shaped, polygonal, smooth slim skimmers pocking and stroking and slicing the water. Thunderhead digs into his pocket, past the burr-ball of string, crab-apples, bone dice, before he finds it – the stone. Igneous, fire-forged, wave sucked and shucked, millions of years in the making, it fits into the crook of his finger like an eye in a socket.

Checkers. Tiddly-winks. Geordie never wins. The Old Viper's an old cheater, an old hornswoggler. She wipes the gameboard clean with an arm like a loaf, sleeves rolled up to the pits. She tips the table till Geordie's kings topple slide and roll under the couch. She dumps the contents of the button bowl into the dog's mouth. *Yelp,* says Porky. Cards spew out of her hands. *Play,* she orders, *maybe letcha win this time.* Geordie stares at the ragged scar line braided like a grin into her neck. *Got a head big as a pumpkin,* is how she likes to describe herself.

Pinkie bops into Putt's for candy. Bax is reading the funnies, gravely, the way most folks read the news. He sighs dolefully and plunges a hand into his shirtfront pocket where he keeps his supply of thumbnail clippings. *Ahem,* says Pinkie. Bax looks up. *Well now, Miss Pinkie, what can I do fer ya? The usual please,* she answers. Bax scoops up a quarter pound of jelly beans, picks out the green and black ones – *I just hate those,* says Pinkie – and pops them into his mouth. Pours the rest into a little sawtooth-topped brown bag and hands them over. Pinkie slaps fifteen cents on the counter, tails up. *Gonna be a contest,* she says, *down on the dock.* Bax, cheeks bulgy as the wind, throws a troubled look through the window that's intercepted by the two-member Miracle Committee passing by, one of them carrying something white in her arms like a baby.

Geordie jumps. From sugary granite to licorice-swirled migmatite to chocolate-coloured mudstone. He hops on the scree from a rock that's a box to one that's a breast to another that's a broken hump of a back. Elflocks flying, eyes peeled. Might be what he needs is down between the cracks. In the loamy damp, where leeches stretch and curl. Where light falling is terror to the woodlice, to the wolf spiders reeling away like small wild hands. Geordie lifts a slab of fossil-choked limestone and *natrix sipedon,* your common watersnake, is wound like a Latin lover beneath. A heavy-bodied, quick-tempered fellow, smiling nonetheless.

Owls hooting in the swamp. Mares' tails twitching in the sky. The Old Viper drags out a dufflebag of silverware. From a tube of toothpaste she squirts out a long blue dangly worm onto the tarnished tines of a fork. Yanks out a shirt that's stuffed into the maw of a chair, rips off a sleeve. Rubs and rubs. Spit 'n polish, that's the thing. Stuff works wonders. Never mind there's *nuthin* to jab. *Nuthin* to cut, *nuthin* to spoon up. Does her shopping in the dump (those dire-eyed ravens, scare your pants off), in the all-night open-air back alley. A bone for Porky, a boot for Geordie. And her so starved she's rooting for something to swallow whole.

Skinned knuckles, nits, and yards of skin about sums up the Meatgrinder. A fat mean kid. Sweaty. Clusters of flies swirl up from his head when he ploughs his fist into things. Opens his mouth for an obscenity to crawl out and there's a fried bologna sandwich with ketchup, half-chewed, smeared like paste on his tongue. Killed every pet he ever owned. Hard to say what the rest of the gang feels for him. A species of affection, but of a low order. Like a neck feels for a goitre. A gut for a pail of pigs' feet.

Stardust under her bed, that's what Pinkie's got. No lion under there, no boogeyman. Just silt from the sky. Luminous dander. Streaming bright angel scurf. Lift the pretty white eyelet ruffle, a wide woman's slip, and have a peek. See. Gold and silver glitter. Sandman stuff, what falls out of Pinkie's eyes in the morning. Maybe somebody's great-great-grandma sifted through the screen and come to rest on her floor like silky-soft talcum. Pinkie goes *hop hop step hop*, chalk dust ghosting her fingers. Unbound bones of sea creatures. Compacted shells and skeletons spelling out of themselves these boxy hopscotch compartments with an arch at the end called HEAVEN into which Pinkie sails.

*Cried to beat all hell,* says Betty Guitar, plonking her bundle down on the counter. *Thunk. Lord yes,* chimes in Daisy Kunkle, *it did. Whole congregation heard it,* says Betty, *you should've been there, Bax. Now, sign here.* She holds up a sheet of paper, a petition with two names on it: Margaret B. Guitar and Daisy Kunkle. One hand wide and loopy, letters like open cages, all sense flown out. The other a minuscule squeezed ant script. Bax gazes, doubtfully (you bet), at the plaster doll-face before him. Red cardinal flower lips, eyes a bird's-egg blue. *People around here got sausage meat for brains,* says Betty. Bax sticks out his chin, scratches it. *This baby* (dumb as stone) *cries out. Well, what's that mean to you, Bax?* Bax chews the inside of his cheek. *Business,* Betty pokes a flinthard finger at him, *big business. Charter buses. Souvenirs. You know, it only takes a rumour, Bax, and they'll be crawling here on their knees.*

Who gets called maggot, scabface, pus-sucker, slimebag? Who's left over, last picked, never picked? Who chucked the rock through the window at school and who got blamed? Who got strapped because he ate the practice cardboard Eucharist? Who kissed the girls and made them spit venom? Who put red dye in the baptismal font? Who's got a no-see-um daddy? A daddy that rises above the roof, that whines through the cracks. That swarms and stings? That casts himself over you like a black sheet? A dissolving daddy? A decomposing daddy? Who is that? Who is it that's always sliding down a snake's tail into trouble?

Thunderhead figures maybe he won't show. *Chickenshit Geordie. Bigmouth. Says he can do it. Yeah, like my dick can yodel. Gonna whip his ass, gonna burn 'im like trash.* Thunderhead's eyes strip the shore, gut the crevices. They probe and slash. Stab into that shack on the hill. (Ugh!) *Old hag! What they say about her?* (What don't they say?) *She do somebody in? Her old man, was that it? Fixed 'im good, they say, buried 'im in the bush. Dogfights somethin' wicked. Made that shack hop, you'd think it was alive.* Thunderhead closes one eye now like he's peering through the sight on a rifle. Lines up Bax in the storefront window, scratching his rear end. Focuses on a little screw-faced idiot kid bouncing around, coiled pigtails sproinging. A blue CCM bike (stolen) whirls into view, wheels flicking gravel. *Ah! Geordie.* Flying down the road to the dock. That rip of a smile appears on Thunderhead's face as he takes aim.

Table set. Foil pie plates to go with the silver. Toilet-paper serviettes. Two gnawed candles rammed into rotgut bottles. Tin of corn syrup, spittle in the freshly licked rim. Hors-d'oeuvres composting on a heaped platter, claw of something or other sticking out. The Old Viper's stomach sets up a howl that sends Porky skittering out the back, a turd on legs. She worries the curtain. Waiting. More waiting. The curtain tears off in her hand like a rag and ends up in the pot on the stove. She tamps 'er down with a broken broom handle, drives it into the boiling belching mass. Then what? She hears a faint *rap rap rap* at the door and moves like a bus to get there. Bowls over a lamp, cord snags around her ankle and she drags it through the room. Two women – one skinny and fidgety, the other fox faced and shifty. Got the Baby Jesus hooked under one arm like a roast. The Old Viper sizes them up. *Well,* she says, *whatchas waitin' fer? Get in here, I won't eatcha.*

Bax is remembering that ventriloquy course they had in the church basement couple years ago. Every Tuesday night it was. Wasn't much in town that couldn't talk then. Dogs, toads, knotholes, you name it and it'd speak to you. Seemed almost everybody had those quivering stiff lips, casting their voices high in the air (sentences like streamers), making moss whisper, and letters before you opened 'em. Ask a question, think you could get a straight answer? No sir. Spend your whole day yapping with a bag of groceries. *So,* Bax says to Bull's Eye St. Jacques, who's leaning up against the counter, lips locked on a can of root beer, *even if it did happen, nobody's impressed. I mean ya need that at least, eh, fer it to count?* Bull's Eye winks his good eye, being birdshit blind in the other. Miracles? Don't talk to him about miracles. Listen, he's cleaning a mess of bass at the fish table this one day. There's a gull hovering overhead, hovering, squawking like a witch, what's it do? Gets him smack in the eye with an exploding guano bullet. Acid it was. Knocks his sight out like a light. *Hey,*

*Bull's Eye, you were there, you hear that baby cry? Naw,* says Bull's Eye, *slep through the whole damn thing.*

*Kersplash!* That's the Meatgrinder's turn. A smacker that lands like a cannon ball. He curses and horks into the lake, narrows his eyes looking for something defenceless to kick – Pinkie, say, who's skipping around snickering into her tiny hand. *Oh, that was good,* she says, *real good* (hee hee), *who's next?* Doggo. A furry-headed fungal hound of a boy. Reminds Pinkie of the muskrat Pop brought home, that she kept in a shoebox until it died and the creepy things came out of the shadows and took it away. Doggo ambles over to take his place at the edge of the dock. Readies himself – no fancy handwork – just hurls his stone straight up. Seems to hang in the air for a splinter of a second before sliding straight down, silent and slick as a raindrop. But it kisses the lake too hard. *Hey, tough luck,* somebody grunts, as ripples tattle circular across the surface.

Shoot the lump. Squeezers. Skat and hearts. Bax's Mama liked all those games. Rounders. Tipcat. Oh, she was a salty one, quick. Out the door, *catch me,* she'd say, *find me.* Never mind the work. Got beat if she didn't do it, and she wouldn't. Garden choked, cows moaning to be milked. Pat and William and Albert, all those damn babies up to their ears in shit. Food dangling off the wall, and consider yourself fortunate if you could get a plate pried loose off the table. *Why, honey, you look like a regular little undertaker,* she'd say to Bax, *don't you know how to cut loose, son?* And *here* she'd tickle him, and *there* she'd be making demon faces, and *find me* she'd say, ducking out of sight. And the babies wailing, and him too. Bawling his eyes out. Imploring her. Running terrified into the yard. Papa coming in from the field, scythe in hand like death itself. And when Bax did find her she was in the well. Face down so he couldn't see if she was laughing at him or not.

Stretch, four feet of swaggering skin and bone, steps forward with a scab-thin shard. Poises himself perfectly. Concentration an electric wire connecting his cat-keen brain to his small deft hand. About to fire, the wad of Double Bubble in his mouth lurches into his throat and gets stuck. His arm goes eely, the shot wild. Grows wings, it looks to Pinkie. Zigzags. Ricochets off the boat house, grazes the water *once, twice* – a chorus counts – *three* times then sinks. No cigar.

Daisy Kunkle lies under the table, a milk-white moustache encrusting her upper lip. Mixed drinks never did agree, and it's no wonder, this one something the Old Viper called a Nurse's Boot (rubbing alcohol and It shoe polish). Betty Guitar's got umbles like iron, though it might've loosened her tongue some. She can't stop rhyming off names: Mal Roberts, Ownie and Warnie McClay, Fran 'Belly' Garret, Bud Priddle, even Baxter Putt. Really now, climbing the hill, she hadn't expected this. A fry pan in the face maybe. If lucky, a hen scratch. A dumb violent signature stabbed onto the petition. But not this chameleon hand forging witnesses, drawing them out of thin air. Ink on paper calling up a whole assembly of believers, making them appear like some kind of black magic.

Victory near enough to poke, Thunderhead approaches the dock's edge. In slow motion, to generate awe. This has to be fully appreciated, remembered. Stalled time turns the air hypnotic, thick as honey. He surges into place. Clothing rippling, muscles, hair stroked by an invisible hand, cruel features gentled into a nobler expression. The stone, black and round as a hole, rides between forefinger and thumb. Arrested on the verge of throwing it, Thunderhead is involved in his own drama like prayer. Then finally, he releases it, and the stone ascends, translated into a weightless unchained piece of the earth. Everyone's gaze trails it, fans it, keeps it up there in the blue sky, keeps it aloft. Until in unison they bring it down, careering into speed, faster, plummeting faster. Gone. It melts into the lake, swallowed without a seam or a scar. But no. *You blew it!* says Geordie. True. True enough. Look again – a lip of water where the stone was taken curls itself into a slight sneer.

What made Daisy Kunkle smile in her sleep, what made the rooster crow and the baby cry, what made Baxter Putt hang his mournful face like a moon in the window, what made Porky whimper, what made Thunderhead and the rest of the gang yowl, what made Betty Guitar and the Old Viper raise seething smoking jamjars of homebrew in celebration, what made the sun falter, what caused those blood-dark clouds to blossom below the surface of the lake, was Geordie. Geordie reaching down his mud-gloved hand and picking up Pinkie's hopscotch marker – an arrowsharp quartzite flake – and tossing it. Carelessly, without even looking. Knowing what? Knowing this time he'd win. Knowing exactly how it would fall. A glinting blade of light – glorious! Impossible, yet slicing the water without a shimmer. Geordie. Lowdown, spat-upon, despised boy, what cut the devil's throat.

TERRY GRIGGS was born and raised in Little Current, Manitoulin Island. She studied English literature at the University of Western Ontario and now lives in London, Ontario, with her husband and son. Her stories have appeared in *Writing, The Canadian Forum, Island, The Malahat Review, Room of One's Own* and *The New Quarterly,* and have been anthologized in *The New Press Anthology: Best Canadian Short Fiction, No. 1, The Macmillan Anthology 3,* and the *Journey Prize Anthology, No. 2.*